BOX

John Locke

TELEMACHUS PRESS

BOX

Cover Designed by: Claudia Jackson
Copyright © Shutterstock/82395196
Copyright © Shutterstock/67333459

Published by Telemachus Press, LLC
http://www.telemachuspress.com

Visit the author's website:
http://www.donovancreed.com

ISBN: 978-1-938701-28-3 (Paperback)
ISBN: 978-1-938701-26-9 (eBook)

Printed and Distributed by CreateSpace
http://www.createspace.com

Personal Message from John Locke:

I love writing books! But what I love even more is hearing from readers. If you enjoyed this or any of my other books, it would mean the world to me if you'd send a short email to introduce yourself and say hi. I always personally respond to my readers.

I would also love to put you on my mailing list to receive notifications about future books, updates, and contests.

Please visit my website http://www.donovancreed.com and contact me so I can personally thank you for trying my books.

John Locke

New York Times Best Selling Author
#1 Best Selling Author on Amazon Kindle

Donovan Creed Series:
Lethal People
Lethal Experiment
Saving Rachel
Now & Then
Wish List
A Girl Like You
Vegas Moon
The Love You Crave
Maybe
Callie's Last Dance

Emmett Love Series:
Follow the Stone
Don't Poke the Bear
Emmett & Gentry

Dani Ripper Series:
Call Me

Dr. Gideon Box Series:
Bad Doctor
BOX

Non-Fiction:
How I Sold 1 Million eBooks in 5 Months!

BOX

Introduction

I

"YOU'VE GOT AN incredibly stressful job," Pigface said. "But that doesn't give you the right to engage in destructive, anti-social behavior."

Pigface, my psychiatrist, knows about my gambling. Knows I've broken into people's homes and assumed their identities while they were on vacation. Knows I've robbed wealthy donors while attending their parties. Knows about the random hookers, strippers, and lap dancers I've dated.

But she doesn't know about the patients I've killed.

Not my *own* patients, of course. They're more innocent than a virgin's sigh.

I kill other doctors' patients.

Not randomly, just those who treated me badly in the past. Maybe this one stole my girlfriend in college, or made fun of me in

1

junior high. Maybe that one cheated on me or ripped me off. Years later they enter my hospital for a routine procedure. They don't re-member me, but shortly after I visit their room, they take a horrible turn for the worse.

They may not die, but they'll suffer.

Just as they made me suffer.

Pigface doesn't know about the patients I've killed, but trust me, she wouldn't approve.

II

THIS IS AS good a time as any to introduce myself.

I'm Dr. Gideon Box, the top cardiothoracic pediatric surgeon in the world. A fancy way of saying I fix kids for a living.

I'm extremely good at my job, but in real life I have issues.

I don't get along with people. I'm antisocial. I don't "mix well." Beyond all that, I've had bad luck with women.

My entire life.

I live alone.

Big surprise, right?

So anyway, Pigface said, "Join an online dating service. Pick one that requires you to fill out a detailed profile, and be honest. Let the experts find suitable matches for you."

She told me to seek women from small towns. Said they'd possess basic core values, be less shallow and self-centered than the women I've tried to date in Manhattan. Told me to take a week off and visit these women. Told me to be positive, keep an open mind.

"What's the worst that can happen?" she said.

So I joined a dating website, spent two weeks narrowing down the candidates, and eventually settled on three small-town Kentucky women: Faith Hemphill, Zander Evans, and Renee Williams. These three seemed to possess the qualities Pigface recommended, as well as the one quality I seek in a woman: excessive horniness.

III

YOU THINK EXCESSIVE horniness shouldn't be a factor? Does the mere suggestion give you the impression I'm thoughtless, shallow, insensitive, selfish?

I fix kids for a living.

Broken kids.

Kids with congenital heart defects so severe, no other surgeon in the world would agree to operate on them. Kids so ill their own *parents* have given up all hope for their survival!

These are the kids they send me.

You think I'm selfish?

I give them everything.

Forty-nine hopeless cases have entered my operating room with zero chance of leaving alive. How many survived?

All of them.

So I'm good at what I do.

But like I said, I have issues.

I cheat death time and again, but not without substantial cost. Death takes a toll on me. On my life.

Death owns my soul.

It's not what you think.

I haven't made a pact with the devil, or anything like that. It's just that I can't stand being me. Can't stand the stress. Can't handle the pressure. Wish someone else could do these operations.

But there's no one.

So four days ago I set out to meet these three women, starting with Faith Hemphill, who lives in Ralston, Kentucky. I flew to Nashville, rented a car, got within two hours of Ralston...

...And met a young waitress named Trudy Lake.

Chapter 1

Trudy Lake.

I'M TRUDY LAKE. Folks here in Clayton think I'm wild.

They're right.

I can't help it. I'm eighteen, stuck in this raggedy-ass, dirt-poor country town, bored half to death.

I waitress here at Alice T's, a teeth-optional greasy spoon located two blocks from Who Gives a Shit, Kentucky. Ninety-nine nights out of a hundred I serve shirtless rednecks in coveralls who smell like whatever they been up to all afternoon. Mostly they come here with fellow workers or drinkin' buddies, in which case they're a back-slappin', nasty-mouthed bunch who take turns tryin' to see who can fluster me most.

It don't work.

I ain't been flustered by man talk since I was fifteen, 'cause I've heard it all. These inbred snuff-abusers are mostly all talk, though some are mean as snakes. And them that are, need to be watched out for, since they been known to lurk in the shadows after closin' time, hopin' to grab a waitress or two.

Just last week, Carrie Miller survived an attack with no worse damage than ripped clothes and sore boobs, but Tootie Green weren't so lucky. Two locals are currently servin' six to ten at Eddy State for puttin' her in a coma last year. Evelyn Sawyer claims she's been raped four times, but I got my doubts, since the subject only comes up whenever she checks into the abortion clinic for what she calls a "tummy tuck."

Evelyn's cosmetic procedures aside, there's often rude behavior to be found outdoors at night. That's why Big Ed, owner of Alice T's, routinely tells the women to holler out if somethin' ain't right when headin' to their cars.

Case in point, last April, Kennon Carlson was gettin' severely crotch bit when Big Ed heard her wailin' out back and laid wood to Gus Wilson's head to the point where Gus walks funny and drools uncontrollably, though he proudly wears the bracelet he made from Kennon's snatch hair he picked from his teeth. Durin' argument season, Big Ed points to Gus's bracelet as proof Kennon ain't a natural redhead.

Sometimes the menfolk show up with their wives and kids in tow. Mostly these wives regard me with mistrust, like maybe they think I'm gonna steal their warts and mustaches or somethin'. While some of the kids are cute in an Easter Island statue sort of way, an outsized number of them walk around town with a mutant, Children of the Corn look about them.

What I'm really sayin', I don't want to wind up like the people I wait on.

I'm still livin' in the house I grew up in. A house so sorry you can fling a cat through any wall without touchin' wood.

I want out. Want to get the hell out of town before the next bad thing happens, which is why I'm payin' middlin' attention to the nicely-dressed doctor at table sixteen on the far side of the room. I'm allowin' him to flirt with me, though he's not much good at it.

Partly it's his age, which makes him automatically sound lame when he talks.

How old is he? Forty, at least. Maybe more.

Reason I know he's a doctor, it's the first thing he said when I brought the menu.

I said, "Hi, I'm Trudy. I'll be your waitress tonight, if that's all right with you."

He said, "Hello, Trudy. I'm Dr. Gideon Box, from New York City."

"Really?" I said. "What kind of doctor are you?"

"I'm a world-famous cardio-thoracic surgeon," he said, proud as punch.

"I guess you got Doc Blanchard beat six ways to Sunday," I said.

"Is that your general practitioner?"

"Yeah, but his degree is in veterinary medicine."

"You can't be serious," he said.

I asked, "Do you have business at the county hospital, or you just passin' through?"

He smiled a goofy grin and said, "That sort of depends on you."

"Me?"

"I notice you're not wearing a wedding ring."

I said, "Neither are you."

Then he looked me up and down and said, "I've met five women prettier than you."

Like I said, he's not very smooth. But I took it as a compliment since his eyes seemed to find a home in my boobs.

We spoke some words durin' the drink order, and durin' the drink bringin', and the food order, the food bringin', and now he's stallin', tryin' to see if his charm's workin' on me.

I can't decide if he's interested in a relationship, or just lookin' to get laid and move along.

If he's truly interested in me, I'll have to sort out my feelin's for him.

On the one hand, he reeks of money, which makes him rarer in this town than a freshly-wiped ass. On the other, while he's not even close to bein' ugly, there's somethin' off-puttin in his manner.

What's the worst that can happen by bein' nice to him?

I'll almost certainly get a big tip. I can live with that. In fact, he already asked, "What's the biggest tip you ever got?"

I had to decide between tellin' the truth and lyin' to get more.

"Twenty dollars," I said, stickin' with the truth.

"That's pitiful," he said.

"Kennon Carlson got fifty dollars once," I blurted out.

"Which one's she?"

I pointed her out.

He said, "She's cute. But she's not in your league."

I rewarded him with my best smile for sayin' that.

If the worst is a good tip, what's the *best* I can hope for out of this doctor?

Jury's still out on that.

But he's been workin' hard these ninety minutes, struttin' his wealth and worldly ways, flirtin' hard, tryin' to impress me.

It's workin'.

I mean, I'm not stupid. He's a man, and men want what they want. It's a fact of life. The trick is makin' them think that what they're gonna get is as good as the thing they want.

It's like that battle we studied in high school, where Robert E. Lee created a diversion. That's what you gotta do when a superior force is about to make its move. And he's a superior force 'cause he's holdin' all the cards. He's rich, he's worldly, he's smart, and he's got a car.

All I've got is my looks.

Around here, looks'll get you any man you want, but Dr. Box is a famous surgeon from New York City. I read somewhere that one out of every ten thousand women is considered movie-star beautiful, and here in Frog Shit County, that's pretty much me. But in New York City the ratio's a hundred times higher, because women who look like movie stars don't strive to live here.

I figure twenty thousand women in New York City are prettier and more sophisticated than me. So I've got to decide if what I've got can compete with what he can get with a phone call.

My advantage is I'm here, and they're there.

Okay, so it's a short-term advantage. Like a one-night-stand sort of advantage.

If this doctor's my ticket out, I can't let him turn me into a one-night stand.

If I let him pursue me, I'll have to put his mind on somethin' else. Somethin' good enough to hold his interest, but different than what he's hopin' for.

Chapter 2

Dr. Gideon Box.

I'M DR. GIDEON Box. Those who know me think I'm crazy.

That's why it's nice to get away sometimes, fly to a city I've never visited before, rent a car, hit the back roads, see if I can fuck a couple of the women I've been flirting with on social media for the past two weeks.

You do this often enough, every now and then you get a bonus.

It's late, you're driving, hungry. You stop at a little hole-in-the wall called Alice T's, in Bum Fuck, Kentucky, whose sign promises "Good Country Cooking!" You go in, expecting the worst, and someone pops up right out of the blue, someone who was never on the radar, someone who turns out to be better than what you were hoping to find in Ralston, Kentucky.

Like the young waitress lingering at my table.

Trudy Lake.

"Nice watch," Trudy says.

I glance at my wrist.

She's right. It's a helluva watch.

"What is it, a Rolex?"

"Piaget."

She nods. "I like it."

"Thanks."

I like it, too. That's why I stole it from Austin Devereaux while attending the party to celebrate his daughter's successful operation.

There's a story here, a great one, but you'll have to take my word for it, since I'm still flirting with Trudy, who is *not* the most beautiful woman I've ever seen.

That's not to imply she's ugly.

It's just that two weeks ago I was in the same room with the two most beautiful women currently gracing the planet Earth: Callie Carpenter, assassin, and Rose Stout, surgical nurse. I've known three other truly gorgeous women: Miranda Rodriguez, courtesan, Willow Breeland, con artist, and Dublin Devereaux, billionaire socialite.

In a group comprised of these five women and Trudy Lake, my waitress, Trudy's sucking hind tit.

Having said that, she's still the sixth most beautiful woman I've ever laid eyes on, and absolutely worth whatever time and effort might be required to separate her from her panties tonight.

She's not very worldly, which works to my advantage. Can't even tell the difference between a Rolex and a Piaget!

I have other advantages. Trudy's a backwoods pony-tailed waitress, I'm a renowned surgeon. She's poor, I'm rich. She appears to possess average intelligence, I'm off-the-charts brilliant.

I know what you're thinking. I'm full of myself, right?

Not true.

I'm a mess.

I'm petty. Mean-spirited. Vengeful. I have a rotten personality. No friends. And a bad track record with women.

I've been flirting with Trudy the better part of an hour. She ignored me at first, but my persistence is paying off. She's appraising me.

"How old are you?" she asks, going straight for the jugular.

I frown. Besides my personality, my age is my biggest weakness. I'm forty-two. She can't be more than...

"How old are *you?*" I ask.

"Eighteen."

Shit. The last eighteen-year-old I dated turned out to be a seventeen-year-old identity thief.

"Eighteen?" I say. "You're sure about that?"

I'd go after older women, but those north of twenty see me coming a mile away.

"Eighteen-and-a-half," she says. "Almost nineteen."

Going the extra mile to make herself appear older tells me she might be interested. But I've been wrong before. In fact, I'm wrong most of the time.

I know one sure-fire way to find out.

I focus my eyes on her chest, and keep them there a long moment before looking up. In my experience, it's fifty-fifty she'll either be flattered or offended. Of course, my success rate is padded by strippers and hookers. What I'm saying, my social skills are so lacking I've offended half the strippers and hookers I've flirted with.

But Trudy's expression reveals nothing.

She looks at her chest.

"Have I spilt somethin'?" she says. "Or are you just bein' a guy?"

"I'm just being a guy."

She nods, but shows no anger, disgust, or any other emotion I've encountered when blatantly fixing my gaze on a woman's chest. Her nod seems to say, "It is what it is. Girls have boobs, guys have eyes."

Maybe country girls are more worldly than I thought.

"What time do you get off?" I ask.

"Ten."

"An hour from now? More or less?"

"You're the one with the fancy watch," she says, then tosses her hair, spins, and heads for the kitchen.

Five minutes later she comes out with a gleam in her eye, looks from side to side, lowers her voice, and says, "Want to do somethin' wild?"

Chapter 3

I HAVE NO idea what a backwoods rural beauty like Trudy considers wild.

Greasing a pig?

Shooting a pig?

Fucking a pig?

"What do you have in mind?" I say.

"Scooter Bing just pulled up out front."

My eyes grow big. "Seriously? Scooter *Bing?* You're *shitting* me!"

She looks puzzled. "You know Scooter?"

I laugh. "I've been in town ninety minutes. I don't know if Scooter's man, woman, or beast."

"He's two of those things."

"Which two?"

"Man and beast."

"And is he gainfully employed?"

"Sir?"

"Does Scooter have a profession?"

"He's our big, fat, deputy sheriff."

"I see. And is there some significance to him having just pulled up outside?"

She laughs. "You talk like a TV lawyer."

I smile, hoping that's a compliment.

She smiles back, waiting for me to say something.

It strikes me how much I love watching her beautiful, expressive mouth form sentences and smiles, and adore how she mangles the English language with her sexy southern drawl. She has a way of taking a monosyllabic word like "Hi!" and making it sound like a full sentence. On the other hand, her conversations require great patience, since they aren't driven by the need to make an actual point. Coming from most other mouths, this round-about style of speaking would annoy the shit out of me. In Manhattan, people say as little as possible and move the fuck along. I like Trudy's world better, where conversation moves slower, and seems to require two people. But it will take some getting used to, and I'm impatient to hear what's wild about Scooter Bing pulling up in front of the restaurant.

She obliges me by saying, "In a minute Scooter will come in, sit at that counter..." —she points to a spot thirty feet away— "and he'll order a cup of coffee."

I say nothing, realizing the slightest comment will delay her getting to the point.

"He'll put a laxative in the coffee. Fifteen minutes later he'll go to the men's room to take a dump."

I can't take it any longer.

"Wow, Trudy. All this time I've felt sorry for you, thinking how bored you must be, living in this little town. And now you tell me this type of excitement is going on all around us?"

She smiles.

It's a helluva smile.

She says, "Before droppin' his pants, Deputy Bing hangs his gun belt over the door of the stall."

"So?"

"He'll have the gun side facin' him, but the handcuffs will be hangin' on the other side of the door."

"And you know this because?"

"It's his way."

"His way?"

"His habit."

"What's the wild part?"

"You're gonna steal his handcuffs."

"I'm *what*? Why the *hell* would I do that?"

"How else are you gonna handcuff me to the chain-link fence out back?"

I cock my head. "You're going to let me handcuff you?"

"Uh huh."

"To the fence out back?"

"Uh huh."

"*Seriously?*"

"Can I be honest about something?" she says.

"Sure."

"No offense, Dr. Box, but it seems to take you a long time to figure things out."

Touche.

But still, this is quite a shock. I've got a history of misunderstanding what women *really* mean when they say what I think I heard. So I risk one more level of clarification, and ask, "What's going to happen when I handcuff you to the fence?"

"We'll find out if I can trust you."

"To do what?"

"Kiss me."

I frown, taking everything she said into consideration.

Then she sweetens the pot, adding, "And I'll let you feel me up."

"No shit?"

"Over my clothes. But that's all."

I look at her blouse a minute, then say, "What about the key?"

"To the handcuffs?"

She opens her hand, revealing a key.

"Where'd you get that?"

"I stole it a week ago."

"And he doesn't *know?*"

"Are you *kiddin'* me?" she says.

"What do you mean?"

"He hasn't used those cuffs in ten years!"

While we look at each other some more a giant man stuffed into a policeman's uniform enters the restaurant and sits at the counter. I check out the cuffs attached to the back of his gun belt.

"Think you can manage it?" she says.

"Of course. I'm a surgeon, after all. So tell me, Trudy."

"Yes?"

"How long can I feel you up?"

"Twenty seconds."

"That's a fast answer. You didn't even hesitate."

"It's a risky thing we're doin'. Twenty seconds seems about right."

"Maybe. But it doesn't give me a whole lot of time to have fun."

"It'll be more fun than not feelin' me up at all. And don't sell the kissin' part short."

"How long will Deputy Dawg be on the toilet?"

"Ten minutes, give or take."

"That should give us at least five minutes at the fence."

"It would," she says, "and I might be so inclined, especially if you prove to be a better kisser than I'm expectin'. But there's a criminal element in town that must be respected."

"What do you mean?"

"You'll be chaining a local girl to a fence. In the middle of the night. Feeling her up."

"Those are good points."

"So are these," she says, indicating her breasts.

We look at each other some more.

"How will I get the cuffs back on his belt afterward?"

She frowns. "I hadn't figured you for such a worry wart."

She turns, and starts to walk away.

"Wait!" I say.

She turns around.

"I'm in!"

She comes back to the table.

"It's best we don't do it," she says.

"What do you mean?"

"It seemed like fun till you started analyzin' it to death. This whole thing probably seems silly to you, instead of wild. You bein' from New York City and all."

"On the contrary, it's extremely wild."

"Tell me why."

"Stealing a policeman's handcuffs while he's taking a shit, and using them to handcuff a beautiful waitress to a fence in the middle of the night and feeling her up—"

She points to her lips.

"—And kissing her, for twenty seconds, then trying to figure out how to replace the handcuffs on the cop's belt without getting caught—trust me, it's plenty wild."

"Well, I wouldn't want to twist your arm, doctor."

"You're not. I'm in. I *love* it!"

"You sure you're up for it?"

"Are you?"

"I'm not only in..." she says.

She leans her hip into me and whispers, "...I'm wet with anticipation."

"Me too," I say to her boobs.

She nods toward Deputy Dawg and says, "Eyes on the prize, Doctor."

"They *are* on the prize!"

Chapter 4

Trudy Lake.

DR. BOX COMES out of the bathroom grinnin' like he's stolen the Crown Jewels.

"What took you so long?" I say.

"I kept retching from the smell."

"That's Scooter," I say. "Let's go."

"You're bringing your purse?" he says.

"I can't very well leave it sittin' there for the riff-raff."

We head out the back door quietly, and I lead him to the eight-foot-high fence that surrounds the dumpster.

"Is this the only fence you've got?" he says, referrin' to the smell.

"It's the only one close by."

"Why's it so high?"

"To keep the deer from gettin' to the garbage."

"The light from the back door makes us easy to see."

"That's why we're only gonna be here twenty seconds."

"Makes sense," he says.

I put my back against the fence and say, "I can trust you, right?"

"About what?"

"Keepin' your hands where I said you could."

"Yes."

"Give me your word."

"You have my word."

I unlock the cuffs, then hand him the key. Put my left wrist in one cuff and lock it. Then put both arms a foot above my head.

"Put my right wrist in the open cuff, and hook it through the chain link before locking it," I say.

He does.

Then he steps back to look at me.

And grins.

Chapter 5

Dr. Gideon Box.

I'VE HANDCUFFED A beautiful waitress to a chain link fence behind a family-style restaurant in Western Kentucky. She's offered me twenty seconds worth of kissing and breast-fondling. Above her clothes.

But there's nothing on earth stopping me from reaching up under her dress, pulling down her panties, and taking her right here in front of the dumpster.

She knows it.

I know it.

Nothing to stop me except my promise.

"You're wastin' time," Trudy says.

I detect a slight waver in her voice. She knows this could go south on her in a hurry. Knows I've got the key in my pocket. Knows I could take her right here, run to my car, and get the hell out of town. She knows I could be thirty miles away before someone finds a tool to cut the cuffs off her.

She starts counting slowly.

"One, two, three..."

"Don't be nervous," I say. "I was just admiring the view."

"Four, five..."

I move in for the kiss. She closes her eyes, puckers her lips.

I kiss her.

Then stop for a moment to look at her angelic face.

She says, "Six, seven..."

But she's breathing heavily.

I kiss her again. She parts her lips slightly, accepts my tongue. Instead of pulling back like most women who kiss me, she murmurs and probes my mouth with her tongue.

I can't believe she's really getting into it like this. What I'm saying, women pretend. With me, it's a routine occurrence. That's because in the real world, women only have sex with me after being softened up with cash, or worn down by liquor or drugs. Women can fake sex. They can pretend they love it, pretend you're the greatest lover they've ever had, you'll never know the difference.

But women can't fake a kiss.

It's too intimate.

Hookers know this. That's why they'd rather give a blow job than a tongue kiss.

Trudy's not faking it.

Her motor's running.

I put my hands on her boobs.

She gasps.

I come up for air.

In a very shaky voice, she says, eight, nine, ten, eleven..."

I'm cupping her breasts.

Through her clothes, of course, but I'm getting plenty of action.

She's right about her "good points." Her nipples are hard enough to poke holes in the vinyl seats of Alice T's dining room.

"Twelve, thirteen, fourteen..."

I kiss her some more, feel her up some more.

She moans.

When I come up for air, she says, "Fifteen, sixteen, seventeen..."

I step back, but keep my hands on her boobs.

"What's wrong?" she says.

I want more. Much more.

She knows it.

"Eighteen..." she says.

I sigh. "You are absolutely adorable."

She smiles.

"Nineteen..."

I move in for one last kiss...

...And wake up in the center of an old, empty barn, tied to a chair.

Two feet in front of me is another chair.

That one's occupied by Scooter Bing, Deputy Sheriff.

Chapter 6

FOUR BATTERY-POWERED camping lanterns have been strategically placed to provide more light than I would have expected them to yield. Two are on the floor, six feet on either side of us, and the other two are perched atop the stall doors.

My head hurts like hell. If my arms were free, I'd feel to see if the lump goes out or in. The answer to that question would help me calculate my odds of surviving the night.

Assuming Scooter Bing doesn't plan to kill me.

"Nice watch," he says.

"Thanks. What did you hit me with?"

"I'll ask the questions, if you don't mind," Scooter says.

He's a massive man. Built like a pro guard or tackle, gone to seed. He's almost certainly wearing the largest cop uniform that can be purchased, but it's clear he's outgrown it. His belly's so big he can't tuck his shirt in.

"How do you even wipe your ass?" I say.

"With doctors."

"Funny."

"You think?"

The old horse barn we're in is empty, save for the chairs and some old boards and paint cans. There's some trash scattered about, scraps of newspaper, a rag or two, and remnants of ancient hay. A moldy cardboard box near my feet appears to have held nails at one time. Not far beyond, a mouse carcass, like Beethoven, is decomposing.

"Nice office," I say. "Or is this your police station?"

"Interrogation room."

"What about an attorney?"

"You got one?"

"I do. And I'd like to call him."

"Would that make you feel better?"

"Yes, of course."

"Then go ahead."

"You've got my cell phone."

"So, call loudly."

I scream for help a few times at the top of my lungs. Then give up.

"Feel better?" Scooter says.

"Yeah. Thanks. What happens now?"

"Normally I'd hang you."

"What's stopping you?"

"I want to hear your side of things."

"And then?"

"And then I'll hang you."

"You got a rope?"

"Trunk of my car."

"You know how to tie a noose?"

"Nope. You?"

"Nope," I say, mocking him. Then add, "Since neither of us can tie a noose, whaddya say we skip the hanging part."

He smiles. "Don't need to know how to tie a proper noose."

"Why's that?"

"It's a seasoned rope."

Chapter 7

"I UNDERSTAND HOW you stole my handcuffs," he says. "How'd you steal the key?"

"Is that your only question?"

"I've got others."

"Can you ask them all up front?"

"Why?"

"It'll save time. That way you can hang me and still have time to get to the county fair before the corn dogs sell out."

"How'd you talk Trudy into goin' out back with you? And how'd you keep her from screamin'? "

"Screaming?"

"When you raped her."

"Whoa," I say. "I never raped her, and you know it."

He gets to his feet.

"Where are you going?"

"To get my rope."

Moments later I'm startled to see the rope he's brought has already has a professional hangman's noose at one end.

"You're going to hang me with a used rope?"

"Why do you care?"

"I've got a thing about germs."

"Trudy's the pride of Wilford County," Scooter says. "Homecoming queen, three straight years."

"I'm not surprised. Were you the runner-up?"

He frowns.

"How'd it go down?" he says. "Trudy's smart. How'd you get her to go outside with you?"

"I tricked her."

"How?"

"I told her I saw a starving cat out back and asked permission to feed him a crab cake."

"And she went with you?"

"She did."

He nods. He can see that happening. Then he says, "When you cuffed her to the fence, why didn't she scream?"

"I said I'd kill her if she made the slightest sound."

"You admit you tried to rape her?"

"I'll admit I *wanted* to."

"Close enough," he says.

He unties the rope around my chest and legs but my wrists are still bound.

"Are these the same handcuffs?"

"Yup. I felt they was appropriate," he says, helping me to my feet.

He places the noose around my neck and tightens it. Then kicks me in the nuts so hard I fall to the floor and nearly pass out.

When I come to, I'm in a world of hurt, gagging, choking. He helps me to my feet and kicks me in the nuts again.

By now my pain receptors are numb with adrenalin, so the pain is palpable. Still, it's enough to make me fall to my knees, retch, and start dry-heaving.

He helps me to my shaky feet a third time, and tosses the other end over a beam I now notice is situated directly above his chair. He makes me stand on the chair, then on top of the chair back. Then he takes up the slack, and ties the rope to one of the stall doors.

"You've got good balance," he says.

"Thanks."

"If you slip, you die," he says.

"Got it."

He watches me a minute, then says, "What sort of name is Box, anyway?"

I start to answer, then say, "Does it really matter?"

"Not really."

He watches me some more, then says, "I can go ahead and kick the chair out from under you if you'd like."

"If it's all the same to you, I'll try to balance a while and see how it goes."

"Any last words?"

"Four."

"Let's hear 'em."

"It was worth it."

"You wanna share what you mean?"

"Trudy Lake was awesome! Her tits are perfect! Feeling her up was one of the highlights of my life!"

"Worth dyin' for?"

"And *then* some! Her nipples were like pencil erasers. Her breath, her tongue, sweet as condensed milk."

"*Condensed milk?* What the *fuck* type of degenerate mother-fucker are you?"

"The kind that would haul Trudy Lake off to New York City and give her ass a daily pounding. I mean, be honest, Scooter. Can you just imagine what it would be like to get some of that?"

"She's barely *eighteen!*"

"Which means I could fuck her for ten years and she'd still only be twenty-eight!"

He comes around to look at me. He's red-faced, furious.

"You're jealous," I say.

"No."

"Then what's the big deal?"

"She's my *daughter*, you miserable fuck!" he yells, then kicks the chair out from under me.

Chapter 8

Trudy Lake.
Thirty Minutes Earlier...

WE HAD A moment at the fence when I wasn't sure I could trust him, but now Doctor Box is kissin' me as if kissin' would put out a forest fire. I'm hooked to the fence and his hands are on my boobs like a blind man huntin' a braille tattoo.

I saw Daddy watchin' us from the bathroom window a minute ago, when I put my back to the fence. I figured he'd let it go. Then again, he questioned our age difference when I pointed Dr. Box out to him while he was drinkin' his laxative coffee.

"Let me get this right," he said. "You want me to let him steal my handcuffs?"

"I dared him to try."

"Why?"

"I'm just messin' with him," I said.

"There are easier ways to land a man, Trudy."

"He's not a man, Daddy, he's a world-famous doctor."

"Yeah? Well I don't like it."

I threw a pout and said, "You never let me have any fun!"

"Fine. Whatever," he said, and left the cuffs where they could be stolen.

When the fun started between me and the doc, I saw Daddy sneakin' up on us. I figured he was just gonna scare Dr. Box and we'd all have a laugh, but Daddy punched him in the back of the head.

"Why'd you hit him so hard?" I yell.

"He was molestin' you!"

"Oh, fiddle," I say.

"Where's the key?"

"In his pocket."

He gets the key out and unlocks me and says, "*Fiddle?* What the hell are you talkin' about, girl? You got more action just now than I did on my weddin' night!"

"You're crazy. Doc Blanchard gets more titty durin' my annual physical."

"If that's true, I'll be payin' him a visit after this."

"Don't be silly. It's a routine medical procedure. And anyway, they're both doctors."

"Does your annual physical with Doc Blanchard include the kind of kissin' I just witnessed?"

I frown.

We're standin' over Dr. Box, who's laid out on the ground like a possum pelt.

"Look what you've done!" I say. "How hurt is he?"

"Why do you care? I'm gonna kill him anyway."

"You'll do no such thing! He's my way out."

Daddy sighs. "Pumpkin, there are easier ways to get out of this town. Plus, you just met him. He's probably married, with six kids."

"He was gonna give me a big tip tonight."

"Let's see."

Daddy goes through Dr. Box's wallet and pockets, finds some bills, counts them out. "How's eighteen hundred sound?"

"He's carryin' that much?"

"He's carryin' thirty-six hundred, to be exact."

"You're takin' half?"

"Seems fittin'."

"Why?"

"He'd bribe me at least eighteen hundred to escape an attempted rape charge, don't you think?"

"I suppose. But I don't want you to run him off, Daddy."

"Trust me, this guy's scum."

"He's rich, and he likes me."

"He may be rich, and he may like you for a night or two, but you need to take this eighteen hundred, get yourself a car, and drive to a better place so you can start a new life."

I frown. "Eighteen hundred ain't but a start for that type of plan. I'd need twice that, at least."

He sighs. "Fine. Here. Take it all. But when you go, don't look back."

"What about Dr. Box?"

"I'll send him packin'. After we have a little talk."

"You're gonna tell him to never see me again."

"That's right. And someday you'll thank me for it."

"What's the plan?"

"Wait here and call Kennon to cover your shift. I'll be right back."

He circles the restaurant to the parking lot, drives Dr. Box's rental car over to where I'm standin'. Then he pushes Dr. Box into the back seat and tells me to drive to Jake Thatcher's old barn.

All the way to Thatcher's, I think about drivin' off with Dr. Box, but Daddy's behind me in his squad car, and I'd never get away. But I'm also thinkin' how I'm gonna write Dr. Box a message about how to contact me after Daddy throws him out of town.

When we get to Thatcher's, Daddy drags Dr. Box inside, handcuffs him, and starts tying him to a chair.

"This where you interrogate your prisoners?" I say.

"It is. Now go out to the car and wait. And do *not* come back in here."

"Can I ask a favor?" I say.

"What?"

"Before you let him go, kick him in the nuts."

"What?"

"Twice. And don't hold back."

"Why?"

"I have my reasons."

"You never fail to surprise me, Trudy."

I do have my reasons. I aim to drive out of town with Dr. Box later tonight, and don't want sex on his mind for at least a day or two while I decide what I want from the relationship, if anythin'.

While Daddy's tyin' Dr. Box up good and tight to the chair, I climb in the rental car and dig a pen and paper from my purse and start writin' him a note. I hear the sound of a trunk slammin' shut and look up to see Daddy carryin' a long rope into the barn. I finish writin' the letter and put it in the console between the seats, figurin' Dr. Box will check to see if there might be somethin' in the console he can use to stop the bleedin' Daddy'll cause durin' the course of his interrogation.

Two minutes passes, then I hear a terrible noise. It's dark, but I can tell half the barn roof has come crashin' down!

Chapter 9

Dr. Gideon Box.

DEPUTY SCOOTER BING kicked the chair out from under me to start the hanging, but the beam couldn't handle the weight, and broke. I fell to the ground. There was a split-second pause before the roof came crashing down.

It wasn't much of a roof, but it was board and tin and heavy enough to kill me. I counted my blessings at having cheated death two times in the space of thirty seconds. As I pulled the rope off my neck, Trudy ran into the barn yelling, "What the hell *happened?* Is everyone okay?"

She saw me moving around and said, "Where's Daddy?"

Turns out Deputy Bing was alive, but his right leg was trapped under one of the rafters. Trudy and I pulled it off him and found his leg was broken.

"Other than that, is he okay?" Trudy asks.

"Yeah, but we should get him to the hospital."

"Daddy?" she says. "You got what you deserve for tryin' to hang my boyfriend."

She unhooks my cell phone from his belt and gives it to me.

"You're not gonna leave me here, are you?" Scooter says.

"I'd take you to the hospital, but sure as shit you'd just wind up throwin' poor Dr. Box in jail. So we're gonna leave now. I'll call an ambulance to take you to the county hospital. And tomorrow I'll call to make sure you're okay. But we're gonna head out now."

She looks at me and says, "Are you fit to walk?"

"I'd be fitter if he hadn't kicked me in the nuts."

Trudy said, "I love you, Daddy."

"I love you too, sugar," he says. "But I'm afraid you've got yourself a bad doctor."

"Time will tell," she says. "Let's go, Doc."

"It's been a pleasure," I say to Deputy Bing as I step over his body.

"She's a good girl," he says. "Don't treat her badly."

I wait till Trudy's nearly out the barn before whispering, "Every time I fuck her I'll think of you."

I get about ten feet before he says, "I'll be sure to tell Darrell you said that."

I stop and turn. "Who's Darrell?"

"You'll see."

Chapter 10

WHEN I EXIT what's left of the barn I notice Trudy's in the driver's seat.

I open the passenger door and lean in.

"Not to be rude, but that man looks way too old to be your father."

"He's had a rough life."

"How old is he?"

"You mean because he looks too old to be my Daddy?"

"Well, yes. To be frank about it."

"He started another family before he met Mom. She was much younger."

She looks at me, smiles, and says, "Guess she was a lot like me."

"In what way?"

"Attracted to older men."

I smile.

She says, "Aren't you gettin' in the car?"

"Who's Darrell?"

She frowns. "Scooter told you about Darrell?"

"Just in passing. Who is he?"

"My brother."

"Will he be mad at me, too?"

"I don't know."

"Should I be worried?"

"No, of course not, honey!"

"Where are we going?"

"Your place."

"I haven't booked a room yet."

"No. I mean, your place. New York City."

"This is a rental car."

"I know. You got it in Nashville. At the airport."

She can tell I'm puzzled, so she adds, "The rental agreement's in the glove box. I read it while waitin' for you. So anyway, I'll drive us to Nashville, we'll catch an early mornin' flight, and be home by noon."

"Home?"

"I've decided to move in with you."

"Seriously?"

"How could I not? We're practically engaged."

I hold up a hand.

"What?" she says.

"First things first."

I open the glove box, pop the trunk.

"What are you doing?"

"I can't leave him like this. He's in pain."

"The man tried to hang you."

"Good point."

"And anyway, we're gonna call an ambulance from the highway, remember?"

"I know. But in the meantime, he could go into shock."

"Is there something you can do to prevent that?"

"My medical bag's in the wheel well, under the spare tire."

"Okay, but let's do this quickly, okay?"

"Why the rush?"

"I don't expect you to understand, but I've tried to escape this town six times and never got past Starbucks. Somethin' always happens at the last second."

"You've got a Starbuck's here in Clayton? No shit?"

"No, of course not. Starbucks is a town, twenty miles south of here."

I grab my bag and a towel from my suit bag, and head back inside. Trudy's a step behind saying, "Who packs a beach towel to go to Western Kentucky?"

"Believe it or not," I say, "Clayton wasn't my destination."

"Where *were* you headed?"

"Ralston."

"Why?"

"It's personal."

"Personal means a woman. It's a woman, right?"

I sigh.

Trudy says, "Good thing you met me when you did."

"Why's that?"

"Whoever she is, I'm way more fun."

I stop a moment to look at her.

She shrugs. "It's true, Gideon."

I say, "In the two hours I've been here, I've been knocked out cold, tied to a chair, hung by my neck to die, and had a roof come crashing down on me."

"So?"

"Where's all this fun you're talking about?"

"Are you always this negative?"

"Yes."

"You know how I see the last two hours?"

"Tell me."

"You had a wonderful home-cooked meal, you French-kissed the Wilford County homecomin' queen, you felt her up, and found true love."

"True love?"

"Well, far as you know."

"What does *that* mean?"

"I got a feelin' about you. And you're about to get me on a road trip. Not many men can say that."

"How many, exactly?"

"Let's just fix my Daddy's leg and get out of here," she says.

As we approach Scooter, he says, "Don't let him touch me, Trudy. He's gonna give me an overdose and kill me."

"Don't be silly, Daddy. He's a doctor. And a damn fine one, too."

"You've only got his word for that."

"I trust him. Now let him give you somethin' for the pain."

As I cover him with my beach towel he says to Trudy, "You know what he said to me a minute ago?"

"What's that, Daddy?"

"He said he was gonna think about me every time he fucks you."

44

She looks at me and says, "You said that?"

I shrug, check his pulse.

She says, "Well, how thoughtful is *that*! Weird, but thoughtful."

She thinks on it a minute, while I check his pupils with my penlight, then says, "More weird than thoughtful, I think."

By then I've given him a shot of morphine. When he seems stable, we head for the car.

Chapter 11

"CAN WE GO now?" she says.

We're in the car again, but this time I'm holding the keys.

"Look," I say. "I appreciate the compliment, I really do. And I understand how things happen at warp speed in small towns. But I met you exactly two hours ago. And while this might come as a shock, I'm not ready to let you move in with me."

"Why not?"

"I don't even know your middle name."

"Leigh. Can we go now?"

I shake my head. "That was a figure of speech. What I mean is I don't know you well enough to take on whatever baggage you might bring."

"Like what?"

"Your father's the deputy sheriff. He tried to hang me just now. And your brother sounds scary."

"All you've heard about my brother is his name."

"The way your father said his name was scary."

"Where's your sense of adventure, Gideon?"

"Sorry."

She sighs heavily. "How long would it take you to know me?"

"What do you mean?"

"I can't be puttin' too much time into this relationship if it's not goin' anywhere."

"It's not so much a time thing."

"Then what is it?"

"I can't just take you out of town with me."

"Why not?"

"I mean, I don't even know if we're *compatible* yet."

"Our kiss didn't tell you that?"

"Sex would say it better."

She frowns. "Are you playin' me?"

"I'm not sure what that means."

"What type of girl would I be if I dropped my drawers for the first guy who offered to drive me out of town?"

"Based on what you said, I might be the seventh guy."

"You're makin' *way* too many assumptions about my last six attempts to escape this shit hole. For your information, I only ran off with one man. The other times were on my own."

"What happened to him?"

"Who?"

"The guy you ran off with?"

"It didn't take."

"Which is my point exactly."

"Again, you're makin' way too many assumptions. The reason it didn't take is because he died."

"Excuse me?"

"He had a heart attack."

"Where?"

"Starbucks."

"The town?"

"The motel at Starbucks. I don't like to talk about it."

"He died during sex?"

"Just before."

"How old was he?"

"Old."

"Like what, sixty?"

"Older."

"Eighty?"

"Let's talk about somethin' else, okay? 'Cause you're really killin' the mood here."

I don't want to talk about something else. I want to ask how long she'd known this octogenarian before he agreed to run off with her. I want to ask if she met him at the restaurant, same as me. I want to know if she made him steal the handcuffs while Scooter was taking a shit. I want to ask if he cuffed her to the fence. I want to know how far he got with her before his heart gave out.

But what I say is, "Tell me where you live, and I'll take you home."

"Call my cell phone first."

"Why?"

"So I'll have your number."

She gives me her number and I call her cell phone.

"This is Trudy," she says. "Who's this?"

"Funny. Where do you live?"

"I'll tell you after you check into the Dew Drop Inn."

"Let me guess. That's your only hotel?"

"Motel. And yes."

"Sounds like a dump."

"A dump would be a step up."

"That's probably not going to work out for me."

"If I come by later, you won't even notice the room."

"Are you planning to come by?"

"I'd like to, but I need to think about it."

"What's there to think about?"

"You ever go to auctions?"

"Sometimes."

"Would you spend every nickel you had on a painting that might be a fake?"

"What's your point?"

"All I've got is my body. If I give it to you tonight, I'll have nothin' left to bargain with. You already proved you're the type of man who expects sex before you'll give me a chance to show what a great girlfriend I can be. I have to decide if you're also the kind of man who'd walk away after gettin' what he wants."

"Nice speech."

"Thanks. It ought to be. I've had a lot of practice givin' it."

"You managed to make it seem normal that I should let you move in with me based on a hot meal and a hanging."

"And a hand job."

"Excuse me?"

"Unzip your pants."

"Uh...shouldn't we call for an ambulance first? For your father?"

She reaches over and starts rubbing me.

"I'll leave that decision up to you, Doctor."

I'm still in pain from the crotch-kicking I received a few minutes ago, but then I remember that sometimes rubbing a sore spot can help the pain go away.

"Scooter should be fine for a while," I say.

Chapter 12

Trudy Lake.

THERE'S AN ART to givin' a good hand job.

Most girls concentrate on the shaft, and feel they need to expend a great deal of energy.

They're wrong.

In my experience, the sweet spots are the head of the penis, and the balls. It's probably eighty percent head, twenty percent balls. You'd be amazed how fast I can get a guy off by rhythmically ticklin' his balls and massagin' just the head of his penis.

Dr. Box is no exception.

I didn't put a clock to it, but let's just say I was shocked to have him explode in less than a minute. And when I say *explode*...

"This has never happened to me before," he gasps. "I bet you could water an acre of land in ten seconds using nothing more than your hand and a garden hose!"

This, from a guy who got kicked in the nuts twenty minutes ago. Not once, but twice.

"How'd you *do* that?" Dr. Box gasped.

"Was it really all that special?"

"Are you kidding?" He turns on the overhead light and says, "Look at the car's interior. If terrorists blew up a *dairy* they couldn't do this much damage!"

He's not lying. If sperm were shrapnel, we'd be dead. Skilled as I am with my hands, I'm a bit taken back by the extent of the coverage. I mean, what type of circus freak has this type of orgasm?

Should I be afraid?

He says, "Honestly. You're so young. How could you possibly be that good?"

I'd rather not tell him I've had three years of practice jackin' off my brother.

I decide to say, "I think it happened like that because we fit so well together."

"You think so?"

"I *know* so."

"Why is that, do you suppose?"

"Do you want me to spend time thinkin' on it now, or do you have somethin' I can clean this up with?"

"I only brought the one beach towel. And Scooter's using it."

"I think we'd need two beach towels for this job," I say. Then add, "Oh, shit!"

"What's wrong?"

I point at the monster truck barreling down the road, headed right for us.

"What the hell is *that*?" he says.

"Darrell."

Chapter 13

Dr. Gideon Box.

I'D NEVER SEEN a monster truck before, except when flipping through channels on TV. And even then I had no concept of the actual *size* until Darrell roared up in a cloud of dust.

"What the *hell?*" I say for the second time.

"You're lookin' at what happens when a redneck inherits a quarter million dollars," Trudy says.

"How tall *is* that thing?"

"Eleven feet. The tires alone are sixty-six inches."

A tall, thin, angry man jumps down from the platform and races to the passenger side of my rental car. He pulls the door open, takes in the scene. Sees my unzipped pants, and what's left of my mighty sword. Sees Trudy's hands dripping with evidence.

"You *whore!*" he shouts.

She slaps his face with a wet, sloppy, smack and yells, "Drive away, Gideon!"

"*Gideon?*" he says. "What kind of pansy ass name is that?"

He tries to grab her. "Get out, Trudy!" he yells. "*Now!*"

"Drive on!" she yells, trying to push him away.

"*Oww!*" she yelps as he grabs her hair.

I fire up the engine and try to figure out how to maneuver around the giant truck. I settle for backing up two feet, and sharply cutting the wheel. But before I can throw the car into drive, Darrell punches Trudy's face, and rears back to hit her again.

"Come here, asshole!" I yell.

He stops in mid swing.

"What did you say?"

"I said, come here, you ugly piece of shit."

"You tell him, Gideon!" Trudy says.

"You'll want to stay out of this, *Gideon!*" he says, making fun of my name. "And don't worry, I'll come over there, soon as I finish dealin' with my woman. Then I'm gonna fuck you up country style. Get out of the car, Trudy."

"*No!* Fuck *you*, Darrell! Drive on, Gideon."

"Yeah," Darrell says, "Drive on, *Gideon,* if you think you can outrun Big Edna."

"You named your truck?"

Trudy screams bloody murder as Darrell pulls her out of the car by her pony tail and throws her to the ground.

"*Help me!*" Trudy yells.

"Help me, *Gideon!*" Darrell says, mocking her.

Instead of jumping out of the car to defend my lady, I put the car in gear and spin out. I fish-tail around Darrell and Trudy, and start to speed away. Darrell runs five or six yards behind me, scream-ing at me, calling me a coward, and so forth, but is shocked when I suddenly throw the car in reverse, floor the accelerator, and plow into him before he has time to react.

I jump out of the car and help Trudy to her feet.

"Are you okay?"

"I thought you ran out on me."

"I had a plan."

"You sure? Or did you improvise after-the-fact?"

"I'm sure."

"Thanks, Gideon. I always had a good feelin' about you."

I decide not to remind her we've known each other exactly two-and-a-half hours.

We follow the monster truck's headlights with our eyes until we see Darrell's body. He's lying in a heap, like a rag doll dropped from a great height. I note the distance from the car bumper to Darrell is a full fifteen feet. I was probably going thirty miles an hour when I struck him.

It suddenly dawns on Trudy he's not moving.

"Oh God, Gideon! Oh, my *God*! I think you've *killed* him!"

We hurry over to him. I take a knee and check his vitals.

"He'll live," I say.

"You're sure?"

"Positive."

"Why isn't he moving?"

"He's moving in slow motion."

"What's that mean?"

"He's suffered significant trauma. It'll take a few more seconds for his brain to catch up. He'll vocalize his feelings soon enough."

"What's that mean?"

"You'll hear him."

"When?"

"Any second."

She does. He starts screaming, crying, rolling around in pain.

"He's hurt bad," Trudy says.

"I won't deny it."

He rolls around some more, but he's fussing about it less. His strength is failing. His energy winding down.

"It's like watchin' cheese slide off a cracker," Trudy says. Then asks, "You sure he'll live?"

"Yes. But it won't be pretty."

"He weren't pretty to start with."

"I'll get the morphine."

Chapter 14

AFTER SEDATING DARRELL, I say, "That was weird, how he called you his woman."

"He's always been protective," she says. "Of course, he's a meth head, so that carries some blame for his disposition."

"It also helps explain his delayed reaction to the pain."

"He earned it," she says. "He's a first-class jerk."

I look at her. "What now?" I say.

"Walk with me."

She leads me fifty feet away from her noisy brother, and uses his truck to block any possible view he might have of us. The monster truck's tail lights are casting a red glow on our faces and bodies.

"How bad is he, really?" she says. "Be honest."

"It was pretty dark, he's clothed, no way to make an accurate diagnosis."

"Best guess."

"Broken ribs, ruptured spleen, internal bleeding, probable multiple fractures in both femurs, assorted bruises, cuts, possible concussion. We should call for an ambulance now."

"No way. Not yet."

"Why?"

"There's a lot to be done."

"Like what?"

"First, zip up your pants."

"Okay."

I zip them and say, "Check. Now what?"

"Now we're gonna get Darrell's work gloves out of his truck."

"Why?"

"Because you're gonna put them on after you do the next thing."

"Which is what?"

"You're gonna give *me* a shot of morphine."

"Why?"

"So it won't hurt so much when you do the next thing."

"What's that?"

"Beat me up."

"*What?*"

"You need to beat the shit out of me."

"*What?*"

"It's the only way."

"I don't understand."

"You saw him hit me, pull my hair."

"So?"

"You've hurt him really bad. He'll probably have permanent injuries."

"I think he had it coming."

"Me too, but he's still gonna have you arrested."

"*What?*"

"We're rednecks, Gideon. He'll press charges, hire an attorney, and sue you."

"On what grounds?"

"He'll say you ran him over for no reason. And Daddy'll say you tried to molest me."

"Daddy's not going to say shit, because Daddy tried to hang me."

"It's your word against his."

"And yours."

"Yes, of course. But he's the deputy sheriff."

"I like our chances," I say. "We can prove the rope brought the roof down. And I can feel the rope burns on my neck."

"And I can see them, even in this light," she says. "So you're right, we're probably okay with Daddy. But that won't stop Darrell from pressing charges and suing you."

"I get that. What I don't understand is why you want me to beat you up."

"We'll have to say you ran over Darrell to save my life."

"That's the truth."

"You know it and I know it. But sometimes the truth needs to be helped along."

"What do you mean?"

"When the sheriff looks at Darrell, and then looks at this little swollen place on my cheek, he's not gonna be convinced you had to run him over."

"What you're saying—"

"You've got two choices. Either beat the shit out of me and I'll tell the sheriff Darrell did it, or we kill Darrell and haul ass out of town."

I sigh. Then, for the third time in a half hour, trudge back to the car to fetch the morphine.

Chapter 15

Trudy Lake.

"I'VE GOT SOME good news and bad," Dr. Box says, after preparing the syringe.

"Bad news first," I say.

"It takes a full thirty minutes for the morphine to take effect."

"Shit."

"I thought you should know."

"We can't wait thirty minutes to do this," I say. "Please. Try not to hurt me too much, or ruin my face."

He says, "I'm uniquely qualified to rough you up."

"Why's that?"

"I'm a surgeon. I understand how to cause the most bruising with the least possible tissue damage. You'll want some heavy bruising, maximum swelling, profuse bleeding in areas that can be easily stitched by a qualified plastic surgeon."

"Try not to sound so enthusiastic, okay?"

"Okay. But you've got to admit, doing this in the dark is an exhilarating challenge!"

When Dr. Box talks like that it creeps me out worse than the way he ejaculates.

"What's the good news?" I ask.

"Good news is, by injecting you now, we'll stay ahead of the pain. When the sheriff and EMS get here I can honestly say you received the injection the same time Darrell did."

"Keep an eye out for Cletus and Renfo."

"Who are they?"

"Darrell's crackhead meth partner twins. If Darrell's here, Cletus and Renfro can't be far behind. Unless they're stoned."

"Is that likely?"

"It's almost a certainty. But just in case."

"Okay. Will do."

She says, "Let's do it. Give me the morphine."

"You're sure?"

"Yes."

"Okay, then. Turn around, bend over, pull your pants down."

"*What?*"

"That's how it's done."

"Bullshit!"

"What do you mean?"

"You didn't inject Daddy or Darrell in the butt."

"It's the fastest, most direct way to administer morphine into the drug stream."

"You're lying through your teeth."

"No. Seriously."

"If you want this relationship to work, you're gonna have to tell the truth."

"I am?"

"Yes, of course. And not just once-in-a-while. Always."

He pauses a minute, then says, "Okay, I'm lying. But how did you know?"

"I was a candy striper for two summers at county. No one got morphine shots in the ass."

"True, because they used a drip."

"Yes. In the arm. Because as any heroin addict knows, the crook of the arm is the most direct route to the pain centers."

"That's never been proven," he says.

"Yes it has."

"Not definitively."

"Arm," I say. "Not ass."

He sighs, gives me the shot. In the crook of my arm. Then he kisses me on the lips.

"I think I'm falling in love with you," he says.

He puts on Darrell's work gloves, takes a step back, and starts punching my face. After a few hits I beg him to stop, but he tells me what I already know, that we've got to really sell it. It bothers me that he's able to keep hitting me when I'm sobbing like this, but I guess it's easier for him because he's a doctor. I'm putting my trust in him not to fuck me up too badly.

But I can't help but wonder if he's enjoying it a little too much.

Finally he stops. Then he grabs me by the neck and throws me down. He helps me up, then carefully hits me in what he calls strategic places to cause bruising and swelling on my torso without breaking my ribs.

Then he does something that surprises me.

He walks over to Darrell, who's unconscious, and makes his hands into fists. Then he slams Darrell's hands into the gravel. He's realized Darrell's fists should look like they hit me more than once.

He comes back to me, puts his arm around me and gives me a hug. By now I'm in excruciating pain. I can't stop crying.

"How much longer before the drugs kick in?"

"Nearly thirty minutes."

"What?"

"I only started hitting you two minutes ago."

"That can't be true."

"Seems longer, right?" he says. "I should call the ambulance now."

He does, then calls the sheriff to report our version of what happened, so I can hear it from start to finish.

When he hangs up I say, "I've got some good and bad news for you."

"Good news first," he says.

"I've got your money."

"What money?"

"Daddy picked your pocket. But I got it back for you by pretendin' I needed it. It's in my purse."

"It is?"

"Yes, sir. The full thirty-six hundred."

He checks his pockets and gives me a funny look.

"I don't want to sound ungrateful," he says, "but I had five grand in my other pocket in an envelope."

I shake my head. "I'm sorry, Gideon. Before the ambulance gets here, you should go through Daddy's pockets."

He takes the money from my purse and stuffs it in his medical bag. Then heads back into the barn to check Daddy's pockets.

He comes back out holdin' the envelope up so I can see it. Then he says, "What's the bad news?"

I sigh. "When the sheriff gets here, and the questions start flyin', you might hear talk of a legal issue."

"What type of legal issue?"

"It's more of a technicality than an issue."

"Does it affect you?"

"Partly."

"Tell me about your legal technicality."

"Well, don't laugh, but legally..."

"Yes?"

"Darrell's my husband."

"*What? Excuse* me? *What?* Darrell's your *husband?*"

"Technically."

"You said he was your *brother!*"

"He is. Technically."

"*What?* But you said...you said—"

"He's my brother *and* my husband."

Dr. Box jumps back like he's come up on a snake. "I've heard of inbreeding before, but *this*—"

"Oh, relax," I say. "There's a perfectly simple explanation."

"This I've got to hear," he says.

I open my mouth to tell him, but then I pass out. Over the next few minutes I go in and out of consciousness. At one point I hear him yell, "I can't *understand* you!"

I try to tell him I'm starting to fall in love with him, but the words seem to float into the air before they get to his ears. I feel like I'm a kid again, in my mother's arms, and she's rockin' me to sleep. When I open my eyes I'm aware I'm lyin' on my back on a bed, in an ambulance. There's a guy sittin' above me, talkin' words I can't make out.

When my head clears a bit, I say, "Where you takin' me?"

"County hospital. You know where that is?"

"Starbucks, Kentucky."

"You been there before? As a patient?"

"Six times."

"Guess this makes seven, huh?"

"I guess it does."

Chapter 16

Dr. Gideon Box.

THE COUNTY HOSPITAL at Starbucks must think they're hosting a family reunion, admitting Trudy, Darrell, and Scooter at the same time for different reasons. I try to imagine the conversation among the emergency room staff at the front desk prior to admitting.

This one was beat up by her husband and brother. This one was run over by his sister and wife's boyfriend. This one had a roof fall on him.

Crazy.

Sheriff Carson Boyd follows me to the Clayton police station to get a statement. Tells his dispatcher to run a check on me. Tells him to do an internet search for good measure.

Three hours later, he says, "Tell me about the letter."

"What letter?"

"The one we found in the console."

"I don't know what you're talking about."

It takes another half-hour to convince him I know nothing about a letter, or who wrote it. Then he leaves the room a few minutes, comes back and says, "You ought to thank Trudy for writing that letter."

"What letter?"

"Let's don't start that again," he says. "Trudy wrote a letter while Scooter was interrogating you in the barn. Her letter corroborates your story, not hers."

"She has a different story?"

"She and Scooter gave different accounts of the hangman's noose we found on the floor, how the barn roof caved in, and how you may have acquired those rope burns around your neck."

"She's trying to protect her father, and he's trying to protect his job."

"Thanks Sherlock, but we'll draw our own conclusions if it's all the same to you."

He follows me to the Dew Drop Inn and waits for me to check in. Then gives me a warning not to leave town.

"I'd like to check on Trudy," I say.

"Did I just tell you not to leave town?"

"It's twenty miles from here!"

"You'll have to wait till tomorrow," he says.

"Is she okay?"

"Why wouldn't she be?"

"Her husband beat her up pretty badly."

"Visiting hours start at eight. Seven if you're family. Tell me you're not a blood relative."

I frown.

He says, "Tomorrow when you visit Trudy at the hospital?"

"Yeah?"

"There'll be a police officer in the room."

"I've got nothing to hide."

"Maybe not. But you're a magnet for trouble like I've never seen."

"You think?"

"Let's review. You're driving through town on the way to Ralston to hook up with a lady you met on the internet named Faith Hemphill."

"That's right."

"You stop at Alice T's for a bite to eat. After dinner you steal my deputy's handcuffs and chain his daughter, our homecoming queen, to the fence behind the restaurant."

"Yes."

"And this was her idea."

"That's right."

"Moments later my deputy catches you feeling up his daughter and somehow gets the impression you're molesting her, so he knocks you unconscious."

I nod.

"They drive you to Jake Thatcher's barn. In the space of twenty minutes all the following happens: One. My deputy ties you to a chair. Two. Unties you. Three. Kicks you in the nuts. Four. *Hangs* you. Five. His daughter—our homecoming queen—willingly gives you a hand job while her father lies on the floor of the barn, unconscious, roof caved in, with a broken leg."

"That's right."

"After the hand job, but before you call the ambulance, Trudy's husband, Darrell, who's also her brother, drives up, pulls Trudy from the car, and beats her up. As this is going on, you pretend to drive away, but suddenly back up and crash your car into Darrell, to save Trudy from further harm."

"Exactly."

"You check Darrell's vital signs, administer morphine, and do the same for Trudy and Scooter."

"Except that I gave Scooter the morphine twenty minutes earlier."

"Before the hand job."

"That's right."

"So before you drive into our sleepy little town, everything's running smoothly. You stop to get a bite to eat, and two hours later three people are in the hospital."

"I was also hung, don't forget."

He looks at my neck, then stares me down and says, "Don't leave town till I say you can."

"Other than visiting Trudy at the hospital?"

"Other than that," he says.

Chapter 17

Trudy Lake.

"STOP INTERRUPTIN' ME," I tell Dr. Box. "My head hurts."

"I'm sorry," he says, "but you're not making any sense."

"Then let me tell it like a story."

"Okay."

"And don't interrupt me," I say.

"Fine. Tell it."

I take a deep breath and say, "Lucy and Lori were identical twins. So alike, even their parents couldn't tell them apart."

"Wait," Dr. Box says. "Twins? They're not related to Cletus and Renfro, are they?"

"Around here, we're all pretty much related one way or other."

"It would be fascinating to chart your family tree."

"Johnny Appleseed couldn't chart *our* family tree!"

I shake the cobwebs from my head and start in again.

"Lucy and Lori were identical twins."

"You've said that three times already. And you've already told me Lucy was your mother."

"Hush! I *mean* it! Or I'll start over."

"Sorry."

"This ain't an easy story to tell, you know."

"I have no way of knowing that. You haven't told me anything yet."

I give him a look and start in a fourth time. "Twenty years ago, before I was born, Lucy, who later became my mom, was livin' thirty miles away, in Rowena. Her twin sister Lori met a guy from Clayton, at a dance. His name was Will, and he worked nights at a convenience store. Lori and Will dated a couple of times, and Lori agreed to a third date, but took sick that day. Will had gone to a lot of trouble to take off work and borrow a car, and Lori didn't have the heart to cancel the date, so she asked my mom to stand in for her. They were supposed to go to the movies, but wound up gettin' drunk. One thing led to another, and my mom had sex with him.

"Did she tell your Aunt Lori?"

"Yes, of course. They told each other everything."

"And Lori was okay with it?"

"She was disappointed, but it's not like she and Will were in love or anything."

"Go on."

"All that week Lori got sicker and sicker. The next week Will got shot and killed durin' a robbery at the store. A month later, mom discovered she was pregnant. Happened the same day Aunt Lori was diagnosed with cancer."

"Whoa. That's a lot to keep up with."

"Wait till you hear the rest. Aunt Lori was dyin', and wanted the joy of raisin' a baby. Mom didn't want the baby. So they traded names."

"What do you mean?"

"Mom had the baby while pretendin' to be Aunt Lori. When Darrell was born, she turned him over to be raised by Lori, and amazingly, Lori's health improved. The next year Mom moved to Clayton, met Scooter. They got married and had me. When I was fourteen, Aunt Lori got sick again, and Mom moved her and Darrell into our home to take care of them."

"How old was Darrell?"

"Sixteen."

"Okay. Go on."

"So anyway, Darrell and I spent a lot of time in the basement and back yard, and started developin' feelin's for each other."

"You and your brother."

"Yes, but at the time we thought he was my cousin."

Dr. Box shakes his head in frustration. "And that would have been *okay*?"

"This ain't New York, where eight million people walk the streets. This is Clayton, Kentucky, where there ain't but a few hundred people my age in the whole county."

"You're saying cousins often fall in love and get married in Wilford County?"

"Well, of *course* they do!"

He shakes his head again.

I say, "You want to go ahead and paint a big red letter on my forehead, or do you want to hear the rest of the story?"

He waves for me to continue, so I say, "No one knew about me and Darrell's relationship, and one afternoon when I was sixteen we

73

ran off and got married and never told anyone. It was a stupid thing to do, more like a joke, you know?"

"This might surprise you," Dr. Box says, "but no. None of this makes any sense to me."

"Well, anyway, we didn't tell anyone. We kept livin' with our parents, kept goin' to school, actin' like cousins. Him, cookin' crystal meth with his friends. Me, workin' part-time at the restaurant. After high school I switched to full time. Aunt Lori got sicker and sicker, and one day her number came up."

"She died?"

"No. She played the lottery. She won four hundred thousand dollars, and took the quarter-million cash option."

Dr. Box shakes his head again and says, "This sounds like a B movie on TV."

"The killer bee movie?" I say. "'Cause that one scared the shit out of me!"

"Please," he says. "Tell your story."

"Well, a week after gettin' the money, Lori dies, and Darrell inherits the money. And that's when we tell everyone we're married."

"That had to be a shock to your mother."

"It was. She hung herself."

"She—*what*? Hung herself? To death?"

"Yup. But not with the rope Daddy used on you."

"That's a relief," he says. Then adds, "Hey, I'm sorry about your mom."

"Thanks. It was tough on us at the time, not knowin' why she did it."

"When was this?"

"Five months ago."

We're quiet a minute. Then I say, "So anyway, me and Darrell got a small apartment, and he squandered his inheritance on a monster truck and lab equipment for his meth business. Two months later, a lawyer showed up with legal papers. He sat us all down and told us the family secret."

"That you and Darrell are brother and sister."

"Right."

"What was your reaction?"

"I moved back in with my dad, got a blood test, filed for divorce."

"And Darrell?"

"He refused to sign the papers."

"And the blood test?"

"He refused to take one."

"So what happened?"

"We got lawyers. A judge finally ordered him to take a blood test." "When did you get the results?"

"Two weeks ago."

"And here we are?" he says.

"Yup. Here we are."

Dr. Box looks like he swallowed a bad hot dog.

"What's wrong?"

"I'm having a hard time picturing you and Darrell."

"In what way?"

"To be honest? Sexually."

"You're still hung up on us bein' kinfolk?"

"I'm odd that way. Are you aware you just asked if I was *hung up* on that issue?"

"It's just an expression, Gideon."

"So is *hanging around*. And *brotherly love*. But in this town those expressions take on a whole different meaning."

I frown at him.

He says, "Even if I could erase the mental image in my head, I find it hard to believe you ever found Darrell attractive."

"Why's that?"

"His size. Shape. Features. Attitude. Complete lack of intelligence."

He turns his palms upward, frustrated. Seekin' an explanation.

I say, "When you're fourteen years old, comin' of age in a small town, proximity is more apt to turn a girl's head than looks, charm, or brainpower."

We look at each other a long moment.

Dr. Box looks sad. Like an old man with heart trouble turnin' down the Tuesday night all-you-can-eat steak special. He wants the steak, but thinks it's bad for him.

I've seen that sad steak look in a man's eyes before.

I say, "You're gonna leave, aren't you."

He nods.

"You're not gonna take me with you."

He sighs. "No."

"Why not?"

He shakes his head and gestures at the room in general, but his meanin' is clear. It's all too much for him.

"I know I look like hell right now, but my face will heal. And when it does I'll be pretty for you for a lot of years. You don't know me that well, but I'll make you a wonderful girlfriend. I can cook, sew, take care of kids and critters. I'm fun when I'm not banged up, and not opposed to grantin' sexual favors. And those favors will belong only to you, Gideon."

"Trudy—"

"I'll be polite to your friends. I won't complain if you drink or stay out at night, long as you treat me with respect."

"*I'll* marry you, Trudy!" the policeman shouts out from the back of the room.

"Mind your own business, Clem!" I scold. Then turn my focus back to Dr. Box. "I see good inside you, Gideon. I'll make you happy."

"I'm sorry," he says. "I can't."

I put on a brave face and sigh.

We look at each other a minute, and I say, "I hope you find what you're lookin' for."

"Thanks," he says. "You too."

He leans over, kisses my cheek, then starts to leave.

"You sure you don't want to *hang* around town a little longer?" I call out to him.

He turns, sees me grinnin', and smiles.

Then says, "Trudy, it's been an honor *hanging* out with you."

"Have a good life, Dr. Box."

"You too, Trudy."

He opens the door, walks through it, closes it behind him.

I stare at the door a while, hopin' it'll suddenly open.

But he's gone.

I start to cry, which makes Clem nervous.

He says, "I can stand outside the door if you like."

I nod.

Chapter 18

CLEM HEADS FOR the door, reaches for the handle, then stops and says, "You're better off without him, Trudy."

I cry some more.

"He's old and weird. You're young and beautiful."

He starts to leave again, then pauses to say, "And somethin' else, if you don't mind my sayin'. It ain't right the way that man ejaculates. Our first thought was a half-dozen baboons had a contest to see who could make the biggest mess, and the answer was, all of them. My personal opinion? There's witchery in it."

I cry harder, and he finally gives up and leaves the room.

Now I can finally read the note Dr. Box passed me when he leaned over to kiss me goodbye just now.

He'd used his body to block Clem's view, and placed a small, folded up piece of paper in my hand that was heavier than it should be.

I open it, and a small key falls out.

I smile through my tears.

It's the key to Daddy's handcuffs. He must have stolen them from Daddy when he went back in the barn to get his money and cell phone.

The note gives a phone number with a two-one-two area code. Then says, *Trudy, I'd run off with you in a heartbeat if I thought you wanted me half as much as you just want to get away. But you can do better than me and we both know it. Last night when I cuffed you to the fence you asked if you could trust me. You can. When you're feeling up to it, call this number and speak to Robert Bothwell, my private banker. I've instructed Robert to wire ten thousand dollars into your personal account every month for the next two years. Now you have a big choice to make: you can finally get out of town, or you can buy your own monster truck! Love, Gideon. PS: I'll never forget our wild and crazy night!*

Chapter 19

Dr. Gideon Box.

PUTTING THE STARBUCKS County Hospital in my rear-view mirror, I work my way to the four-lane highway that leads to Ralston, Kentucky.

I'm not breaking the law.

Sheriff Carson Boyd left me a text message, saying I could go on about my business. It read: *I spoke to your boss in NYC, Mr. Luce. He says you're easy to find if I need you. Plus I want you the hell out of my town. So go on about your business. Somewhere else.*

So that's what I'm doing.

Taking my business to Ralston, Kentucky, to meet Faith Hemphill.

What can I tell you about Faith you don't already know?

Very little.

I barely know the woman.

It's a two-hour drive, so let's start with what I've learned from the dating site.

If her profile's accurate she's my age, forty-two, recently divorced, with a daughter in college. She lives on a ranch. If the photos she posted are actually her, she's attractive, or was at the time they were taken. She's a custom saddle-maker, which sounds interesting, doesn't it? I mean, she works with leather, right?

Riding crops?

Bondage collars?

That's sexy, isn't it?

I'm not sure. But it's an angle to explore.

I try to picture her naked, on all fours. I'm riding her, whacking her fanny with a riding crop.

Wait.

Riding her?

I'm having trouble with the mental image.

I can't picture how to hump her and smack her ass at the same time. I'm not sure it works anatomically. And anyway, I don't like the idea of hitting a woman.

I know what you're thinking.

I didn't have any problem hitting Trudy last night.

Good point.

I'll admit there was something amazing about beating Trudy up last night. I think it had to do with her insisting that I hit her, and knowing I *had* to hit her, and the certain knowledge that hitting her would benefit both of us. It's like the world's biggest taboo, hitting a woman, but we both knew it had to be done.

It was like getting a free pass.

I have no doubt that given the opportunity, Darrell would have beaten her half to death. Or all the way to death, since he was furious about the divorce, and the judge's ruling, and the thought of losing Trudy forever. At the very least he would have done serious, and possibly permanent, damage to her face, nose, eyes, or teeth.

But I ran him over before he had time to do that.

Then I punched Trudy's face and torso.

Hit her hard and often.

Big man, right?

I did it the safest way possible, but feel weird reporting it wasn't half as unpleasant as I would have expected. Maybe it's because beating her up solved all our problems. It kept me out of jail. Ensured her divorce would sail through the court system. Allows her to get a restraining order against Darrell. Puts him in line for a jail term, which could very well save his life.

You think I'm stretching things saying that beating Trudy could save Darrell's life?

Think about it.

What type of life expectancy does Darrell have in the meth business? This guy's a Grim Reaper trifecta: a meth cooker, meth dealer, and meth addict all rolled into one.

I try singing it out loud, in my car: *I beat a girl and I li-iked it!*

Katy Perry, eat your heart out.

All jokes aside, I didn't enjoy it, and I'd never do it again.

But it wasn't *that* bad.

For me, anyway.

I drive another twenty minutes and decide I really miss Trudy. And not just because she let me beat her up.

I miss *her*.

Why did I give her all that money after knowing her a single night?

Because I'm a nice guy?

No.

Because I feel guilty for beating her up?

Partly.

But if I'm being honest, the main reason I gave her all that money is because I *can*.

It's chump change to me.

Go ahead and hate me for saying that.

Elvis was known for giving women Cadillacs just for being pretty. Does that make him a great guy?

It does?

Well I'm not a great guy. I just think Trudy's a great girl who deserves a break.

What I'm saying, I was extremely wealthy *before* one of the world's richest men paid me a hundred million dollars to perform an unauthorized surgery on his girlfriend. How much is a hundred million bucks? The interest *alone* pays me a hundred grand a week!

I'd like to see *you* try to spend that much money without doing something nice for someone along the way.

Of course, by removing Trudy's money issues, I've removed the only reason why she could possibly be interested in me. So I go back to visualizing Faith Hemphill naked on all fours. This time she's wearing one of her custom-made saddles on her back. I expect (and hope) I'm too big to ride her and switch her ass with a riding crop, so I visualize someone smaller doing it.

A few months ago I met a midget, a dwarf, and an elf at a government facility near Bedford, Virginia.

At least I think Charlie's an elf.

I picture Charlie riding Faith Hemphill, switching her ass with a half-sized riding crop.

"Giddyup!" he shouts. He whacks her rear flank. "Trot!" *Whack!* "Canter!" *Whack!*

I shake away the image. It's doing nothing for me.

My mind drifts back to Trudy Lake. She was all bruised up, in the hospital bed, telling me what a wonderful girlfriend she'd be.

I believe her.

I had an eighteen-year-old girlfriend a few months ago.

Well, that's a stretch.

She wasn't my girlfriend, I was paying her for sex.

Wait. That *is* a girlfriend.

But anyway, it was a great relationship.

For me.

Maybe Trudy would be willing to live with me a while for a fee. She could bank the gift I give her each month, and I'd handle her expenses.

I have half a mind to turn the car around and see if Trudy might be interested in this type of relationship. You know, until she can find a nice guy. My guess is no, but it's worth asking.

Except that I'm about to turn off the highway onto Leeds Road, which puts me less than two miles from Faith Hemphill's ranch. I've come all this way, I should at least meet her.

As I start my turn I see a car broken down on the side of the road a hundred yards ahead. It's an isolated area, and this guy clearly needs help. His hood is up, his wife is sitting on the ground, holding a baby. He's waving at me.

My plan is to pretend I don't see him. I'm a New Yorker, so this is status quo for me.

But this guy won't be denied!

He sees me and suddenly starts jumping up and down and flail-ing his arms in a way that makes him impossible to ignore. He's actually stepping into my path on the road, putting himself in danger, determined to flag me down. A guy this determined has to be in serious trouble.

But I view this situation the same way I view religion.

If your religious beliefs bring you joy and comfort, I'm happy for you. Because the world needs good, positive people who believe they're here for a purpose. To me, the best of the bunch are those who get involved and willingly help others.

There are good, solid, decent country people all over this fine state. And I believe almost anyone who lives in this isolated area would be thrilled to stop and help this poor family. They wouldn't think twice about the hassle, the heat, the inconvenience, or the blood or vomit that might wind up getting on their car seats.

Since I'm *not* like these people, I don't want to deprive those who are. Doesn't it make sense this family should be helped by those whose joy in life is to help others?

I think so.

I flip him the finger and keep going.

As I drive toward Faith's house I decide I don't really want to see her. What I really want is to drive back to Starbucks County Hospital and spend the rest of the afternoon sitting with Trudy, keeping her company. We'll talk, laugh, and get to know each other better.

That's what I'd like to do.

But what if Trudy doesn't want me?

I'd be driving all that way only to be turned down.

She's probably already asked Robert Bothwell to wire the first ten grand to her personal account. If so, he's already explained she gets the money whether or not we're a couple. By now she's come to the conclusion the money's enough. She can finance her new life and find a good man closer to her age. That would be in her best interest.

But you know what I'm thinking right now?

Trudy's young and impressionable. And I might be able to talk her into a relationship that would be in *my* best interest.

To put it another way, Trudy's worth fighting for.

She's absolutely worth fighting for, and I'm willing to drive all the way back to Starbucks to see if I can find some common ground that would give us a chance to be together, even if it's only temporary. If necessary, I'll spend all evening trying to convince her. Then, if she still doesn't want me, I won't badger her. I'll accept her decision and move on.

I wonder if I'm starting to fall in love with her.

God, I'd hate to lose Trudy tonight.

Of course, I'd feel a lot better about losing her if I fuck Faith Hemphill first.

Chapter 20

Darrell Lake.

"WHAT DO YOU mean he drove right past you?" Darrell yells into the phone. "You should've flagged him down!"

"I *did* flag him down," Cletus says. "I jumped up and down and waved my arms and got halfway in the lane."

"That's bullshit. If he'd a' seen you, he would a' stopped."

"He saw me, all right. Gave me the finger."

"*What?*"

"He looked at Maisie and the baby sittin' on the ground, then looked at me, swerved *into* me, to force me to jump off the road, then flipped me the finger as he went by."

"What the fuck kind of doctor does a thing like that?" Darrell says.

"A bad one, you ask me."

"*Now* what're we gonna do?" Darrell says.

They pause, thinking about it.

"It was such a simple plan," Darrell says. "He pulls over to help you, you bash his head in, and rob him."

"And make sure he's dead before drivin' off," Cletus adds.

"That's right. We're eighty-six hundred richer, and he can't run off with my wife."

"Sister."

"Whatever."

Cletus says, "You sure he's got that much cash on him? 'Cause that's a lot of cash."

"Accordin' to Scooter he's got five grand and Trudy give him another thirty-six hundred this mornin'. 'Course, Trudy might a' lied about that part. But even five grand's a lot of money. And he'll have drugs in his medical bag."

"We still know where he's headed. And I still got Maisie and the baby with me, if that helps."

"Are you really that stupid?" Darrell says.

"What do you mean?"

"That's a doll, not a baby. And there is no fuckin' Maisie."

"Right. I know that. I'm just sayin', me and Renfro can keep pretendin' to be husband and wife, with a baby. If it helps. So what do you want me to do?"

"Let me think on it a minute and call you back."

Chapter 21

Cletus Renfro.

IF YOU'RE OUT in the middle of nowhere, thirty miles north, east, or west of Clayton, Kentucky, and happen upon an old, beat-up motor home, and the fumes coming out of it suggest someone inside might be conducting illegal, non-agrarian chemical experiments, you've likely stumbled on Darrell Lake's mobile crystal meth lab. And if you're dumb enough to get close enough to holler the name Cletus Renfro, it won't be one person shooting at you, it'll be two.

Because Larry and Tulie Renfro named both their twins Cletus.

Not that they looked the slightest bit alike, one being a girl and all.

The problem was the parents were told by the ultrasound lady at the hospital that Tulie was going to have a boy. Larry and Tulie fought like cats and dogs over the name. Larry was fond of Clem, Tulie wanted Brutus.

Their arguments went far beyond the type you'd find in civil homes. By the time Larry and Tulie compromised by taking three letters from each name, to arrive at Cletus, only three teeth remained attached to Tulie's gums, and Larry had lost all feeling on his left side.

It was Larry by day with his fists, Tulie by night with her frying pan, and they surely would've killed each other had it not been for Social Services who threatened for the first time in Wilford County history to take someone's children before they were even born!

Even so, theirs was an uneasy truce. So incendiary was this issue of names, when Tulie popped out the second child, Larry said, "Fuck it. Name that one Cletus, too."

"But it's a girl," the doctor said.

"I don't give a shit," Tulie said. "They'll both be Cletus, and they can work it out on their own."

Growing up, it didn't matter to the twins what they were called. But their first grade teacher insisted the girl have her own identity, so the female Cletus said, "Call me Renfro."

And that was that.

Renfro Renfro?

Why not?

But the kids at school called her Cletus anyway, and that's what stuck. Except that Cletus continues to call his sister Renfro, which pleases her. Of course, when she's pissed at him, she pushes his buttons by calling *him* Renfro, which makes for classic, and interesting, arguments.

Cletus and Renfro toss the fake baby in the trunk and climb in the car to avail themselves of the air conditioning.

Only to find it's broken again.

He starts the car up.

"What're you doin'?" she asks.

"Darrell said Dr. Box is courtin' a woman, Faith Hemphill. Figured we'd drive to her house and stake it out."

"And you're goin' there now?"

"I thought I would. If we roll down the windows we'll get some air circulatin'."

"And you're just gonna head on over there right now."

"That's right. You got a problem with that?"

"Can you see out the front window at all?"

He looks.

He can't.

The hood's still up.

She laughs.

"Shut up, Renfro!" he says.

"*You* shut up, Renfro!" she snaps back.

Chapter 22

Dr. Gideon Box.

I'M AT FAITH Hemphill's, counting the misrepresentations.

First, she lives in a ranch *house*, not on a ranch. There's a lot of acreage surrounding her house, fields, scrub pine...but none of it belongs to her.

Including the ranch house.

She rents.

So the first misrepresentation is there's no ranch. And the house itself is old and dilapidated. When I crossed the front yard to the porch a few minutes ago, a two-headed cat climbed out from under the car port to meet me, which I took to be a bad sign.

The second misrepresentation is Faith is larger than her photos indicated.

Much larger.

To put the size differential into perspective, if the Faith in the photos is a penny, the Faith I'm staring at is the piggy bank it goes in. This is a large woman. She could use sheep for tampons.

The third misrepresentation is she's half-again older than she claimed.

That, or she's had a helluva rough life.

On the other hand, she's pleasant-looking, and seems nice. I won't pretend she'd transition smoothly into the Manhattan club scene, but I don't hang in those circles anyway, so that's not an issue.

For me.

Having said that, I *could* fit in with that bunch if I wanted to, and Faith could not.

I'm sitting in her cramped den, drinking home-made lemonade, squinting hard, trying to recognize her from the photos on her profile page.

She's not the same woman.

Period.

We're making small talk.

"Nice watch," she says.

"Thanks. Nice..." I look around, trying to find something to compliment. And come up with, "Nice taste you have. In watches."

"Why, thank you!" she says. "What is it? A Timex?"

"Piaget Altiplano."

"Is that Italian?"

"Swiss."

"I love Swiss cheese," she says.

"Who doesn't?"

She sees me eyeing her and says, "I may be a little curvier than you expected."

No shit? A little curvier? You think?

"Those pictures were taken a few months ago, and I've put on a couple of pounds since then. But I can lose them back, stay the same, or put on some more weight, if it suits you."

I look at her and think I've figured out where all the lost pounds go from other people's diets. In the same way elephants have been known to travel many miles in order to die at the elephant graveyard, lost pounds find their way to Faith Hemphill's ass.

My smart ass remarks aside, I don't mind her being heavier than she advertised, and I don't mind her lying about the photos. I don't care that she embellished her lifestyle by claiming to live on a ranch. The fact I've been in her home a half hour and no one's tried to hang me yet is enough to keep me content.

"What was it that attracted you to my profile on the dating site?" she says.

The truth? Her web name.

Horny Hottie.

But what I say is, "You seemed interesting."

"In what way?"

I start to say something about her ranch, and horses, then realize ninety percent of her profile might be a lie. So I say, "Tell me about your saddle business."

"Well, aren't *you* the eager beaver!" she says.

"Huh?"

"If you want to see my horses, just *say* so, silly man!"

"You have horses?"

She winks.

"Where are they?"

"*You* know where!" she says.

I'm confused. Does this mean she *doesn't* have horses? Or she *does*, but they're somewhere else?

She says, "The horses I'm referrin' to can be found right where you'd expect."

"Which is where, exactly?"

"In my bedroom, of course!"

I raise an eyebrow. Could "horses" be a euphemism for something sexual? And do I *want* to do something sexual with this older, plus-sized saddle-maker?

I think about Trudy. If I knew for certain she wanted me, I wouldn't even consider entering this woman's bedroom. I suppose I could call Trudy and ask her if she wants me, but that would be rude to Faith.

"Ready to see my horses, cowboy?" Faith says, adjusting her bosoms.

I still can't imagine what she means.

Horses?

In the bedroom?

Weird.

Then again, I suppose it can't hurt to at least find out what she's talking about.

"I'm ready," I say. "I think."

She smiles, takes my hand, helps me to my feet, leads me to her bedroom. When we get close, she says, "Put you ear to the door and listen."

I do, and she says, "You hear it?"

I *do* hear it. But have no idea what I'm hearing. Some sort of humming or buzzing sound. Like the sound a giant neon sign makes when you're standing beneath it. I'm also detecting an occasional gurgling, bubbling sound. The kind half a dozen stoners might make while smoking water pipes at the same time.

I briefly wonder if she could possibly be running an opium den in her bedroom.

She puts her palm on my cheek and says, "Once you enter this portal, your life will never be the same."

"That sounds rather hyperbolic," I say.

"Just you wait," she says.

Then she opens the door.

And my jaw drops.

Chapter 23

IT'S NOT WHAT you think.

    Meaning, it's not what I thought.

    Nor what anyone would think.

Chapter 24

FAITH HEMPHILL HAS seahorses.

Hundreds of them.

In tanks, covering every square inch of wall space in the room.

The tanks are different shapes, sizes and colors, but all contain seahorses.

"Pick a favorite," she says.

"There are hundreds. It would take me all day."

"Welcome to my world!" she says.

Then—I shit you not—she starts introducing them to me, one-at-a-time.

"This one's George," she says. "And this here's Lucas. That's Gracie. And this little guy's Jimmy. Hi, Jimmie!" she says. "There's Lucy, and...and...there's Desi, and Fred."

She focuses harder. "Where's Ethel?"

She searches the tank. "Ethel?"

She looks at me. "Where's Ethel?"

"I don't know. She was here a minute ago," I say, trying to be funny.

"You think that's funny?" she snaps.

I shrug.

"Oh!" she says. "Thank God! There she is, behind the seaweed. See her?"

"Uh huh."

"Ain't she glorious?"

"Stunning!" I say, though I can't tell one from another.

"This one's Betty, this one's...oh, my goodness!"

"What now?"

"Elizabeth."

She turns to me again.

"Elizabeth hardly ever comes to this neighborhood!"

"Fascinating," I say.

"You know what I think?" she says.

"What's that?"

"I think she likes you."

"How can you tell?"

She smiles, then changes the subject. "Guess how much these tanks and seahorses are worth?"

"I have no idea."

"Guess."

"Five thousand dollars."

She laughs. "I didn't ask you what you think I invested. I asked what you think they're worth. These are all mine. I started with a hundred. Each individual horse was hand-picked from a reputable breeder."

"Hand picked?"

"Yes, of course. They're registered."

"You're joking."

"Not at all. The cheapest horse in these tanks would sell for eighty dollars. And the tanks run a thousand dollars each."

"Are you serious?"

"I am."

"In that case they must be worth—" I try to do the math. "Seventy-five thousand dollars?"

"Closer to eighty-five."

"So, you raise them and sell them for a profit?"

"I never sell my babies till they die."

"Excuse me?"

"I'll tell you more about that in a minute."

"Are they hard to keep alive? Hard to care for?"

She gives me a look. "Are *babies* hard to keep alive? Are *babies* hard to care for?"

"Human babies?"

"Yes, I'm asking you about human babies."

"I'll go out on a limb and say yes, human babies are hard to care for."

"You're damn right they are!" she says. "And seahorses are far more fragile than human babies."

"How so?"

"They're susceptible to disease and bacteria. And they can't be left alone, even for a day."

"That sort of describes human babies too, doesn't it?"

"Are you *serious*? Human babies can be left alone for *days* in a temperature-controlled environment."

"You know this from personal experience?"

"I do. I used to run a daycare. But that was in a different life. These days I never leave my horses for more than four hours at a time. If you want to take me out, give me notice, and have me back in four hours."

"Glad you told me."

"If I'm gone they won't eat. If they go twenty-four hours without eating, they die."

"Ever thought about getting an automatic feeder?"

She snorts. "You don't know shit about seahorses, do you?"

"Not really."

"Would you use an automatic feeder for a baby?"

"A *human* baby? My gut reaction is no."

"Damn right. And automatic feeders don't work for seahorses, either."

"Because?"

She frowns. "Are you for real? Automatic feeders? For *seahorses?*"

"I feel stupid for suggesting it."

"Well, don't beat yourself up about it. You'll learn. Wait till you start scrapin' 'em!"

I look at my watch. "Oh, shit!" I say.

"What's wrong?"

"I had no idea it was almost noon! Darn!"

"Don't even *think* about leavin'," she says.

Chapter 25

FAITH HEMPHILL SAYS I can't leave? That's a bad sign, don't you think?

"Why can't I think about leaving?" I say.

"I haven't finished introducin' you to my horses yet! And you sure as *hell* don't want to miss what happens after the introductions!"

"What's that?"

"Are you familiar with Chinese herbology?"

"Shockingly, no."

"What sort of doctor *are* you?"

"A *real* one."

"Well, for your information, Doctor Smart Ass, dried seahorses are one of the most potent aphrodisiacs in the world."

"Do tell."

"When my horses die, I hold formal funerals. After the ceremonies I dry them and grind them into powder and sell the powder for a hundred dollars an ounce. Plus postage."

"To whom?"

"People on the internet."

"You're telling me there are people who actually pay money for dried seahorse powder?"

"I make nearly fifty grand a year from the powder alone."

"I thought you were a saddle-maker."

"I am. I make saddles for seahorses."

"Shut...*up!*"

"It's true! Afterward, if you want, I can show you my work-shop."

"Afterward? After what, exactly?"

She winks. "Let's just say my gentlemen friends come from miles around just to drink my home-made lemonade."

"*What? Why?*"

"It'll take forty-five minutes to introduce you to my horses. By then you'll have the most ragin' hard-on you ever experienced in your natural-born life!"

"You drugged my lemonade?"

She looks shocked.

"*Drugged?* No, of course not! I *enhanced* it. Think of Viagra...on steroids!"

"You put a dead, ground-up, dried seahorse in my lemonade?"

"I sure did!" she says proudly. "And not just *any* seahorse, mind you. That was Wilbur, one of my all-time favorites."

"Wilbur?"

"That's right. And see these?" She grins and points at her smile.

"What, your teeth?"

"Yep."

"What about them?"

"They come out."

"I don't understand."

"Oh no? Well, you *will!*" she says, looking at my crotch, licking her lips.

"I don't think so!" I shout.

I turn and bolt out the door, run to my car, dig the ipecac syrup from my medical bag.

I know what you're thinking.

Most doctors frown on using ipecac to induce vomiting these days.

True, but that's because most people want to vomit after ingesting a known poison. Ipecac doesn't work for most poisons. But if you're in Crab Crotch, Kentucky, and want to get dried, dead seahorse out of your stomach in a hurry, ipecac's the choice I'd recommend.

Unfortunately, it takes up to twenty minutes to work, so I grab a small plastic bottle of hydrogen peroxide, rush back into Faith's house, and mix it in a cup of lukewarm water. Then I puke my guts into her toilet. When I open the door, Faith is standing there, hands-on-hips, with a sour expression on her face.

"What the hell are you *doin'?*" she demands.

"What's it look like?"

"Looks like you puked Wilbur into the toilet."

"That's *exactly* what I did. What the hell's *wrong* with you?"

"What are you *talkin'* about?"

"You're feeding people *seahorses?* Are you *insane?*"

"You got a problem with seahorses? Because if you do, we're not gonna get along."

"Are you aware seven million people in the continental United States are allergic to shellfish?"

She frowns. "Seahorses are fish. Not shellfish. Look it up."

"They *eat* shellfish. Then they die. Then you serve them to people."

"No one's died on me yet."

"How do you know? You sell the powder online. Five hundred ounces a year! You've probably killed *dozens* of people!"

"That's ridiculous. The FDA would've been all over my ass if that happened."

"Have you ever heard of vibrio vulnificus?"

"No, but if it has anythin' to do with my vulva, you're shit out of luck unless you get on my good side, and quick. Because you're killin' my mood faster than herpes in the bean dip."

"Vibrio is bacteria found in seawater."

"Good thing I ain't sellin' seawater!"

"Seahorses are notorious for carrying vibrio."

"Oh, pooh."

"Pooh?"

"I'm notorious for carryin' a *gun*," she says. "But that don't mean it's *loaded*."

Suddenly the front door explodes from its hinges and crashes to the floor.

A man and woman enter.

Shockingly, I recognize them.

They were on the side of the road earlier, trying to flag me down.

What I didn't see the first time around is the gun.

Chapter 26

"WHAP HAPPENED TO the baby?" I ask.

"We ate it!" the man says. "How's *that* for an answer?"

"Sadly, it was on my short list of probable responses," I say.

"Heard you felt up the homecomin' queen," the woman says.

I wonder how it's possible that sixteen hours ago I felt up a waitress in Clayton, Kentucky, and it's already common knowledge in Ralston, two hours away.

"You felt up another woman?" Faith says. "You told me your car broke down!"

"Did he tell you he ran over a man and tried to run off with his wife?" the man says.

Faith looks at me.

"Get out of my house," she says. "We're through!"

"Neither of you are goin' anywhere," the woman says. "Except in a pine box."

The man picks the door up and props it against the frame to block the view from the road. Not that anyone would be driving this remote stretch of road in the first place.

"Sit down," he says.

I frown. "Why?"

"So I can shoot you, you dumb shit."

"Look," I say. "I realize I didn't stop to help you a few minutes ago. But don't you think you're overreacting?"

"Am I, motherfucker?"

"It's just an observation," I say.

"Shoot him where he stands, Cletus," the woman says.

He turns on her.

"What did you just call me?"

"Sorry. But when you kill 'em it won't matter I used your real name."

"What if I was just plannin' to scare 'em, and steal their money?"

"I didn't say your last name was Renfro, you dumb shit."

Faith and I look at each other.

Cletus cocks his gun.

His companion says, "Wait. Get his money first."

"Why? It'll be easier to go through his pockets when he's dead."

"You might get blood on your clothes. Ever seen CSI?"

"Of course I have. I aint' stupid."

"Then get the money first."

"You get his money. I'll hold the gun on him."

While they're sorting out who's going to do what, Faith flings something at them that explodes into a giant ball of smoke.

They scream, cover their eyes, and fall to the floor, shrieking.

What the fuck?

The gun hits the floor, discharges, and shoots the woman in the leg. Blood spews from her wound like water from a sprinkler head, which tells me the bullet lacerated her blood vessels. She'll be dead within a minute. Faith makes a move for the gun, but the woman finds it first, and starts shooting blindly, while writhing in pain, until she's out of bullets.

Five shots, five direct hits.

All into Cletus's body.

Faith and I look at each other again.

"I'm not cleanin' this mess up by myself," she says.

Chapter 27

"WHAT THE FUCK was in that smoke thing you threw at them?"

"My home-made blindin' powder."

"Where was it?"

"I just killed two people," she says. "Who were about to kill us."

"So?"

"So this is what you want to know? Where I keep my powder?"

"Yes."

"In my dress."

"Where in your dress?"

"In the back."

She turns around and shows me a pocket in the back of her dress. I'm a little concerned to see another packet in there.

"What sort of person carries around bags of powder that can blind people?"

"The sort who lives in the middle of nowhere and has a business to protect."

"Have you ever used it before?"

"Not the permanent one."

"What does that mean?"

"I make two kinds of powder. Bad and worse."

"What's in the worse one?"

"Soot, seeds and dust."

I give her a look. "I don't think so."

She smiles. Then says, "That's all it is. Soot, seeds and dust. Ask me what kind."

"What kind?"

"One-third soot from a wood fire, one-third ground up ghost pepper seeds, one-third glass dust."

"What's ghost pepper?"

"Extract of Naga Jolokia chili peppers."

"I'm not sure you're pronouncing that correctly."

"Does it really matter?"

"Not really. You get those around here?"

"I buy 'em from a customer runs the Fire Festival in Albuquerque."

"The Fire Festival?"

"It's an annual chili pepper event."

According to Callie Carpenter, the assassin, Naga Jolokia is one of the hottest chili peppers in the world. When distilled into a powder it registers two million plus on the Scoville heat index, which makes it more potent than the pepper spray used by police. But when you add ground glass to the mix? And soot?

Holy shit!

Those components attack not only the eyes, but the lungs as well. Faith's little smoke bomb could have killed both intruders on its own.

"How would one go about obtaining a supply of glass dust?" I ask.

"A friend of mine works nine hours a week at the glass factory, polishin' glass with a belt sander. He collects it, meets me twice a month, we trade dust."

"Dust," I say.

She grins.

"We trade spit, too, if you want to know. And other bodily fluids."

"I should probably go," I say.

"You're my witness, doctor."

"Seriously? Because this looks like a simple case of breaking and entering."

"I'd prefer to have a witness."

"But I'd do you more harm than good. I've already been in trouble with the Clayton, Kentucky police department."

"For feelin' up the homecomin' queen?"

"That, and running over her husband."

"You really tried to run off with her?"

"I considered it, but things didn't work out."

We look at the dead bodies a minute, then she says, "I'll make you a deal. If you promise not to report me to the FDA, I'll let you walk."

"I'm a doctor."

"So?"

"It's my duty to report what you're doing with this seahorse powder. It's dangerous."

"I just saved your life!" she says.

"I agree. Thank you."

"Don't that give me a pass in your eyes?"

"It's a matter of ethics."

"Ethics," she repeats.

"That's right."

"Tell me somethin', doctor."

"What?"

"How many people could die from what I sell?"

Before I respond, she adds, "Be honest."

"How many could *die*?" I say. "Or get sick?"

"Die."

"Worldwide?"

She nods.

I think about it a few seconds. Then say, "A dozen a year. More or less."

"A dozen a year," she snorts.

"More or less."

"And how many are gonna die from smokin' cigarettes?"

"That's hardly the same thing."

"Humor me."

"This year?"

"Uh huh."

"Worldwide?"

She nods.

"Six million."

"Six *million*?"

"More or less."

"Uh huh. And how many will die because of doctor fuck ups?"

"There's no way to determine the world-wide statistics for death by medical error," I say.

"In America, then."

"Two hundred thousand. Possibly more."

"Not less?" she says, sarcastically.

"What's your point?"

She says, "Do you really give a shit if my powder kills twelve people in the world this year?"

I think about it.

"Not really," I say.

Chapter 28

Cletus & Renfro.
Fifteen Minutes Earlier.

"DID HE LEAVE?" Darrell says, answering his cell phone from his hospital bed.

"Nope," Cletus says. Then adds, "You takin' a shit?"

"What?"

"Sounds like you're takin' a shit."

"I'm in pain you dumb bastard. This is what pain sounds like. I was fuckin' run *over*!"

"Still, the way you're gruntin' and all, you know what it sounds like? To me?"

"Yeah. It sounds like I'm takin' a shit."

"Yeah."

"Now that we've worked that out, if Dr. Box is still in the house, why are you callin'?"

"I was thinkin' about changin' the plan."

"Why? Didn't you already clog his exhaust?"

"Nope."

"Why not?"

"I haven't got around to it yet. Plus, I'm tryin' to think of somethin' I have that'll do the job. I was thinkin' of usin' my shirt, but I might need my shirt."

"The plan was to shove somethin' up his tailpipe. He'll drive his car a few miles, you follow from a distance, his engine shuts down, you pull over, rob him, shoot him, and drive on."

"I know. But he could be in this bitch's house all day."

"So?"

"It's hot, and our air conditioner's broke. And we've got customers waitin' on product we ain't even cooked yet."

"What's your idea?"

"Bust through the door and start shootin'."

"Kill 'em both?"

"She might have some money, too. That'd make it look like a real robbery."

"What about the neighbors?"

"She lives out in the boondocks. Leeds Road. It's like, a mile to the nearest neighbor."

"Sound carries in the country. Especially gunshots."

"Yeah, but the neighbors ain't there."

"You checked?"

"Their farm's all boarded up. Got a sign on it."

"If she's all alone in the boondocks, she's probably got a shotgun or somethin'."

"She wouldn't be holdin' a shotgun while visitin' with the doctor. More likely, they're fuckin'. We can bust in there, kill 'em both, get the cash."

He pauses. "Wait a minute."

"What now?"

"He just come runnin' out the house."

"The doctor?"

"Yeah."

"You said he's runnin'?"

"He's at the car. Doin' somethin' in the trunk."

"Can he see you?"

"Naw. He seems upset."

There's another pause. Darrell says, "What's he doin'?"

"Runnin' back in the house."

"Is he carryin' somethin'?"

"If he is, it's small."

Darrell laughs. "It's small all right. Just like his dick."

"You seen his dick?"

"No, you dumb shit. I'm just sayin' he probably ran out to the car to grab a condom."

"He's gonna fuck her?"

"Sounds like it to me."

"So we can bust through the door, surprise 'em, shoot 'em while they're fuckin'?"

"Yeah. Shoot 'em right there in the bed. Or wherever they're fuckin'."

"I hope they're fuckin'."

Darrell says, "Me too."

"Why?"

"It'll make your job easier, and I'll enjoy seein' the look on Trudy's face when she hears her precious doctor got shot while fuckin' another woman."

"What if they ain't fuckin'? Can I still bust through the door and kill him?"

"Yeah, go ahead. But if he's not lyin' down on the bed, be sure to sit him in a chair before you shoot him."

"Sit him down?"

"Yeah."

"Why?"

"You ever shot a man, point blank before?"

"I've shot *at* 'em, from inside the truck."

"Well, it ain't the same thing. A man thinks he's about to be shot might jump outta the way, or throw somethin' at you or do all sorts of crazy things. You get him sat down, it limits his movement. It also contains the blood spatter. Sit him down, then shoot him. Got it?"

"Got it."

"Say it."

"I'll sit him down, then shoot him."

"Don't miss."

"I've got six shots."

"Save a couple for the woman."

"If I run out of bullets, I'll beat her to death."

"You like the idea of leavin' evidence at the crime scene?"

"What kind of evidence?"

"The kind you leave when you beat someone to death."

"No."

"Then shoot her. From a distance."

"How far?"

Darrell sighs. "You think it's possible she's got two chairs in her livin' room?"

Cletus looks up at the house. "Yeah, it's possible."

"Sit her down, just like you're doin' with the doctor. Then shoot her, too."

"Sit 'em both down at the same time?"

"If possible."

"Then shoot 'em from a distance?"

"Yeah. But not too far, or you'll miss."

"How's ten feet sound?"

"That's fine. Call me when you're done. And don't steal any jewelry or personal items that can be traced back. Just cash. Nothin' else."

"What about the shotgun?"

"No guns, no stereos, wallets, purses, credit cards...wait. I'm not gonna give you a list of what not to steal. Just don't steal anythin' 'cept the cash they got in their pockets."

"Got it."

"Anythin' else?" Darrell says.

"Yeah," Cletus says, winking at Renfro.

"What?"

"Enjoy your shit!"

"Fuck you!"

Chapter 29

Dr. Gideon Box.

IT'S NOT THAT I don't trust Faith Hemphill, I just want to hedge my bet because the best intentions can go out the window when detectives swarm a crime scene. So I drive nine miles toward civilization, find a truck stop with shower facilities, and use them. Then I change clothes and brush my teeth twice and use mouthwash till it makes my eyes water. Because if there's one thing I've learned from this experience, puking up a dead seahorse has a negative effect on your breath.

After cleaning up, I enter the truck stop restaurant, order a sandwich, and make sure I'm seen.

Then I drive to Faith Hemphill's house and pretend I've just shown up for our date.

Of course, the cops try to move me along before I can even park the car.

"What's going on?" I ask.

"Move along, buddy. This is a crime scene."

"Is this Faith Hemphill's house?"

"Who are you?"

"Dr. Gideon Box. I'm supposed to be meeting her. Is she okay?"

"Pull over there and park," he says, pointing to a vacant spot on the road.

He follows me there, takes a pen from his pocket, opens his notebook, and says, "Let's hear your story."

I give him my name, address, phone number, show him my driver's license, and tell him about my email correspondence with Faith. Tell him I'm here for our date.

"Does she know you're coming?"

"I called yesterday and told her I'd try, but I wasn't sure I could make it."

"Why not?"

I shrug. "Cold feet. Fear of rejection. You know."

He frowns. "You've seen her photos?"

I show him the photos I downloaded on my cell phone.

"That ain't her," he says. "If I were you, I wouldn't worry about rejection. Come on. I'll introduce you."

He leads me to the side of the house where Faith is being questioned by a couple of detectives. When she sees me she raises an eyebrow, but says nothing.

"You know this man?" my police escort asks.

"You're Dr. Box," she says.

"I made it after all!" I say. "Is this a bad time?"

The detectives, the cop, and Faith all look at each other and start laughing. Then Faith says, "You missed all the excitement."

"What happened?"

She looks at the detectives. They nod. She says, "Two meth dealers broke into my house. I threw some powder in their eyes and they shot each other to death."

I stare at her without speaking.

"Some date, huh, Doctor?" my cop says.

"You should probably go," Faith says.

"Nice meeting you," I say.

"Maybe we can try again another time," she says.

The cop escorts me back to my car.

"You don't look so good," he says.

"Huh?"

"Are you okay to drive?"

I nod.

"There's plenty of fish in the sea, Doc."

"Excuse me?"

"I'm just sayin', she ain't the only starfish in the sea."

I wonder if he's using these analogies because they're common expressions or because of Faith's seahorse collection.

He says, "Listen, Doc. If you're into chubby girls, I've got a sister you should meet. She's been workin' on herself."

"In what way?"

"She's lost fifty-five pounds, fixed up her hair and wardrobe, even bleached her mustache."

"Her mustache?"

He looks around to make sure no one else can hear him. Then says, "That ain't the only thing she bleached!"

He winks at me, then leans in again and whispers, "She bleached her *asshole*! You ever heard of such a thing?"

I shake my head.

"I were you, I'd check that out!"

121

"Because?"

"It's as white as a lily," he says.

"You've *seen* it?"

He winks.

Have I fallen so far that a small town cop thinks I'd be interested in a chubby girl with a mustache who's so proud of bleaching her rectum she showed it to her brother?

"She sounds charming," I say. "But I might need a little more time. I'm not sure I'm ready to date yet."

He nods. "Can't say I blame you."

I drive away quite pleased with myself. I'd told Sheriff Carson Boyd I was heading here to meet Faith Hemphill. If word got back to him I showed up around the time two people were shot to death he might think it a bigger coincidence than it was.

I pull over to the side of the road and check my cell to see if Trudy's called.

She hasn't.

I call her, but get no answer.

While I've got the phone out, I pull up a photo of Zander Evans, and fire up the GPS to see how long it might take to drive to Paducah.

Then I view another photo of Zander Evans, and think, *Why not?*

Chapter 30

ZANDER EVANS IS the youngest and prettiest of the three dating site women, and the most determined to have me visit. She promised me "a hell of a good time" if I ever came to town, and punctuated it with a big "Woohoo!" I think women who write "Woohoo!" are more likely to give oral, don't you? I mean, you can't even say the word without making a circle with your mouth.

Zander said we'd hit the riverbank, listen to music, drink wine, make out, "and see what develops." Normally I'd be all over that, but I wanted to visit Faith first, since she lived the furthest away. Then hit Paducah, and finish up in Logan with Renee Williams, whom I consider to be a sure thing.

Fifteen minutes of driving gets me to a place where I have to make a decision. Straight ahead takes me to Starbucks.

Left leads to Paducah.

Do I literally stay on the straight and narrow and hope for a future with Trudy? Or veer left for a river romp with Zander?

I turn left.

Then feel guilty enough to pull over and call her again. But again, there's no answer. Now I wonder if she's okay, so I call the hospital and use my best doctor voice to confer with one of the nurses, who tells me Trudy's fine, she's just groggy from the pain meds. So I'm thinking I could drive two hours and sit in Trudy's room all afternoon and she might not even know it, or I can hop over to Paducah to see if Zander Evans still wants to take me to the riverbank.

Faith looked nothing like her photos. But I know for a fact that Zander does, because we Skyped.

She even did a little dance for me.

Thinking about that dance makes me want to speed up. But I fight the urge. It's only forty miles to Paducah, and I'd rather not have to deal with any more small-town cops, or hear about their sisters.

All three dating-site women are on my speed dial, so I press Zander's name, and she answers on the first ring.

"Two-one-two area code!" she says. "It's really *you*! Hi, Dr. Box!"

"Call me Gideon."

"Okay, Gideon! What's up?"

"If you still want to see me, I'm not far from Paducah."

"No *shit*? How close *are* you?"

"Forty minutes."

"Wow! Okay, I won't complain about the short notice, but gosh, this is cutting it close! Okay, look, I'm going to hang up and get myself in order. You should've called sooner! Hey, Doc? I mean, Gideon?"

"Yes?"

"Do me a favor?"

"What's that?"

"When you get to my exit, turn left. After a mile you'll see a junk yard on the left side of the road. Pull into the entrance and give me a call. I'll give you directions from there."

"You want me to park in a junk yard? Is it safe?"

She laughs. "This isn't New York, Gideon! The junk yard's run by a sweet little old couple in their eighties. But you don't have to turn in, just pull in the entrance and call me."

"Okay."

"I better hang up now. But Gideon?"

"Yeah?"

"I can't *wait* to see you!"

I don't get that reaction very often. As you might imagine.

"Really?" I say.

"Really. I'm going to show you a great time today!"

"I'm looking forward to it!"

"You won't be sorry. I'm in a great mood!"

"Thanks, Zander."

"A *great* mood, Gideon! See you soon!"

"You got it," I say, quite pleased to have finally made a good decision when it comes to a female.

I know what you're thinking.

Something bad's going to happen at the junk yard.

How did you get to be so jaded?

Chapter 31

NOTHING BAD HAPPENS at the junk yard. In fact, something great happens.

Zander's standing there, waiting for me!

Looking...amazing!

Not in Trudy's league, mind you, but damn cute.

Nice, tight body, decent face, great hair.

She climbs in the front seat.

"Nice watch," she says.

"Thanks. It's a Piaget Altiplano."

"And it cost more than my house, didn't it!"

She's carrying an enormous handbag that appears to be filled with clothes.

"Are we spending the night somewhere?" I ask.

"You never know!" she says, giving me a wink. Then says, "Can I kiss you real quick?"

"Yes, of course. Why?"

"Because I *want* to!"

"Seriously? That's great! I just meant, what made you ask that?"

"You know how first dates are. As a guy, you probably spend half the time wondering, 'Should I kiss her? If so, when? After a couple drinks? After dinner? At the end of the date? In the car? At her doorstep?' It's a pain. You might not even get around to kissing me at all because you're not sure if the moment or the mood's right."

She's right. I never know when to try to kiss someone on the first date. From the slaps alone it's obvious I guess incorrectly most of the time.

Zander says, "I want to get that part over with, so we can concentrate on the fun."

"Works for me," I say.

We kiss right there on the gravel entrance to the local junk yard.

It's an okay kiss. The kind I'm used to.

The fake kind.

Again, Zander's not in Trudy's league. But how many women are?

And how much can I really expect from a first kiss *before* the first date?

I'm quite pleased to be kissed at *all* at this point, and the fact she wanted to start in with a kiss gives me high hopes for the date.

"Where's your car?" I say, looking around.

"I caught a ride," she says.

"Why?"

She looks down.

Says nothing.

"Is something wrong?"

"I'm embarrassed."

"Why?"

"You're a rich doctor from New York City. You live in a penthouse. You have a *doorman!*"

"So?"

"There aren't any penthouses in Paducah."

"Of course not."

"No doormen."

"So?"

"The truth is, I was ashamed to let you see where I live."

"Don't be silly!"

"I'm sorry, Gideon. I just didn't want you to judge me based on that."

"I would *never* do that."

"Well, maybe later, then."

"I look forward to it."

She removes two jugs of wine from her handbag.

"This isn't what you're used to, but it'll loosen me up."

"Sounds perfect!"

She says, "You're probably wondering why I covered the wine with clothes."

"I hadn't thought about it, actually. But since you brought it up, tell me."

"McCracken County's dry."

"What's that mean?"

"No alcohol. Paducah's a wet city in a dry county."

"So alcohol *is* allowed?"

"In the city. But if we venture past the city limits we'll need to keep it hid."

"That's crazy."

"That's Kentucky," she says. "New York's different, I bet."

"Very. In lots of ways. But there's something charming about being in small town Kentucky."

"You are so full of shit!" she says, laughing.

I smile.

She says, "So, you still want to go to the riverbank, get to know each other better?"

"I'd love to."

"Me too. Can we make a quick stop along the way?"

"Of course."

I know what you're thinking.

Something bad's going to happen when we stop. That *is* what you're thinking, right?

Chapter 32

I'M IN THE car by myself.

Nothing bad has happened.

Zander has a girlfriend named Chris who works at the local bowling alley. She wanted to swing by, visit with Chris a minute.

"Chris's husband died recently," she told me on the way here. "I'm going to invite her to come with us, if that's okay with you."

She saw the look on my face and laughed.

"Look at you," she said. "I was *kidding!*"

"You were *kidding?*"

She laughed some more. "Of *course!* You think I'd drag you all the way here and bring a grieving widow with us to a make-out party?"

"I *hope* not!"

"It's too bad you feel that way, because Chris has a huge crush on me and asked if we could have a threesome at her place later to-night."

"Seriously?"

"Again, I'm kidding. Only this time you didn't seem as upset. You think I'd share you with another woman? Are you crazy?"

"At this point, I'm not sure what to think."

"Good. That means I've got you right where I want you."

"Where's that?"

"Confused."

"I'm definitely confused," I say. "So, are we going to the bowling alley or not?"

"We are. At least, *I* am. I *do* need to visit Chris. But just for two minutes. And no, she's *not* coming with us!"

Zander directed me to the bowling alley, had me pull around to the back of the building, park by the employee parking sign. She got out, knocked on the door, and a young lady opened it, waved at me, then let her in. I remained in the car as directed, and have been here about five minutes.

There are no cars out front, so either it's a dying business, or they're not open yet. Chris must have inherited a Ford 150 from her husband's estate, because that's the only other car here.

Another five minutes pass quietly, then Zander comes out and climbs in the car.

"Everything okay?" I say.

"Peachy."

"Good. How do I get to the make-out spot?"

She laughs. "You mean the riverbank?"

"Yeah."

"Keep going straight till I tell you to turn."

I follow her directions.

Ten minutes later, we're one of a dozen cars on the side of the levy, angled nose-down, toward the river.

"We're not alone," I say.

131

"In two hours there'll be thirty cars and trucks here. People come from miles around."

"To drink?" I say.

"Drink and fuck," she says.

"I like it."

She opens a jug of wine, tilts it to her mouth, swallows three times, then hands it to me and smiles.

"Now you drink some, so we'll taste the same."

I take three sips.

It's rancid. Like someone started with a bad jug of wine and pissed in it to improve the flavor. But I'm careful not to wince. I don't want to offend this young, good-looking girl while parked in a sacred place where people come from miles around to drink and fuck.

She takes another chug, then leans over, kisses me, and says, "How far does this seat recline?"

Chapter 33

IT'S A RENTAL car, so I have no idea how far the driver's seat reclines. Nor do I know which button makes it happen. So I start pressing buttons like crazy till I find the right one. When I do, I hold it down till the seat stops moving. By then it's touching the back seat.

"Lie back and close your eyes," she says.

"What are you planning?" I ask.

"You'll see, soon enough."

I know what you're thinking.

But who cares? Just let it happen, okay?

Chapter 34

ZANDER UNBUCKLES MY belt, pulls my pants down to my ankles.

"There goes your first line of defense," she says. "Now all that's between your body and my mouth is your underwear."

"What if someone walks over to the car?" I say. "Or pulls up beside us?"

"That won't happen."

"Why not?"

"People around here carry guns. You sneak up on another car, you're begging for bullets."

"You're sure?"

"Trust me. Now, where was I? Oh yeah, I remember!"

This seems too good to be true.

I'll grant you that.

But remember, I hand-picked these women because they claimed to be sex-obsessed.

You might think Faith Hemphill was a bust, but she had a sexual plan for me that included introductions and an aphrodisiac. I declined *her* advances. True, Faith's appearance was shabbier in person than online, and Zander's *exactly* as she appeared online. But is it *that* big a stretch to believe Zander might find me attractive enough to offer a blow job so quickly?

I hear a sound, like she's rummaging around in her handbag.

"Keep your eyes closed," she says.

"What are you doing?"

"Looking for a condom."

"You won't need that."

"I won't, huh?"

"I'm clean. Seriously."

"You know how many times I've heard that?"

No. And I don't want to. But now that the thought has been placed indelibly in my head, I can't shake it. It's like telling someone not to picture a banana, or a giraffe.

There's no way around it.

Images and questions flood my brain. How many guys has she blown on the riverbank? Has she been treated for STDs? How many times? Sobering thought: oral sex is a pipeline for gonorrhea and herpes. Does Zander have herpes? Aids?

My eyes are still closed, and I'm trying my best to ignore the doubts in my mind, but I'm suddenly feeling a lot more room in my underwear than there was a moment ago.

Zander notices it too.

"What's happened?" she says.

I open my eyes, lift my head slightly as she does what I wanted her to do seconds ago, except that now it's humiliating.

She pulls my underwear down.

But instead of caressing my manhood, she stares at it.

And frowns.

I shake my head, trying to will myself larger. I close my eyes. Lie back. Try to think sexy thoughts.

But all I can think is how she's staring at me, wondering where my dick went.

"Gideon?" she says.

"I'm working on it," I say, but we both know it's a lost cause.

She waits patiently for minutes while I strain to achieve an erection. But I've killed the mood. To her it's as romantic as waiting for her constipated grandfather to push a pellet into the toilet at the old folks' home.

"Maybe if you touch it," I say.

She sighs.

I wish she hadn't sighed. Now I feel like a charity case.

God, I hate myself sometimes!

I had it made!

She uttered one lousy comment about wanting to use a condom, and I suddenly imagine all sorts of terrible things about her. What the hell is my problem? Did I think I was her first?

I sit up.

We look at each other.

This is as awkward as it gets.

"Maybe you just need to pee," she says, cheerfully.

Bless her heart! She's given me a graceful exit. I can pee, or pretend to, regain my composure, come back aroused, ready to roll. She understands this.

"Is there a bathroom nearby?" I ask, pulling up my pants.

She points to a stand of trees a hundred yards away and says, "Boys go there." Then she uses her thumb to indicate a spot behind us and says, "Girls use the bushes on the other side of the hill."

"Do you need to go?" I say. "I'll be glad to wait for you."

"I'm trying to decide if I need to or not."

She closes her eyes a second, then says, "I think I'm okay. I used the bathroom at the bowling alley a little while ago."

"Okay, then," I say. "I'll be back in three minutes."

"You want to take the keys with you?"

It dawns on me for the first time the car's been running since we parked. I check the temperature gauge. It's fine.

"I don't want you to get too hot," I say. Then laugh.

"What?"

"Wouldn't it be funny if you stole my car?"

"No. It would be terrible. And why *wouldn't* the thought cross your mind? You don't know me that well. You should take your keys. I'll be fine till you get back."

"I trust you completely," I say.

"Thanks, Gideon. That deserves a kiss!" she says.

I kiss her and say, "Thanks, Zander."

"For?"

"You know."

She smiles. "Hey. It can happen to anyone. We'll make up for it in round two."

I kiss her again, then get out of the car to pee. It takes a minute to find a secluded area, which I need, because I actually *do* have to piss. Guess I was too excited to notice.

Halfway back to the car I can already tell she's gone.

She's either bailed out on the date or decided to pee after all.

I go with the good thought. After all, she could have stolen my car, and didn't.

She's gone up the hill to pee. I'm sure of it.

Otherwise, why give me all that encouragement, and offer a kiss? If she planned to bail, she'd just bail.

Back in the car I consider pressing the button to raise the seat, but decide against it because I want to be ready when Zander returns.

I'm more comfortable with the riverbank scene now. I think part of my problem was worrying someone was going to walk up on us, despite Zander's reassurance to the contrary. But as I look around I can see that all the cars and trucks are maintaining a respectful distance from each other.

I lie back and close my eyes. Try to imagine Zander naked, but it's not helping me. She hasn't given me enough to go on yet, nudity-wise, so I let my thoughts drift to Trudy Lake. I didn't see her naked, either, but I touched her partially and she touched me thoroughly. I remind myself I had no problem staying erect with Trudy working the controls.

These thoughts of Trudy are doing the trick. I allow my hand to graze my crotch.

I graze it again.

I feel my plumbing start to work, and help it along with a gentle bit of rubbing.

I'm interrupted by a sharp tapping on the window. I grin, expecting to see Zander, proud of what I've accomplished while waiting for her.

But it's not Zander, it's a policeman.

Chapter 35

"GREAT GOBS OF goose shit!" the cop shouts. "What the *fuck* do we have here?"

My first thought is to hide the wine, in case we're out of the city limits. But I don't see the wine.

"Don't just lie there, tryin' to coax the fillin' outta your Twinkie!" he roars. "Sit the fuck up and roll down the window!"

I press the window button, but nothing happens.

It suddenly dawns on me the car isn't running. I glance at the steering column.

The keys are gone.

As is Zander's giant handbag.

I open the door.

"Get to your feet and lean against the car, maggot."

I do as he says. He pats me down.

"Empty your pockets onto the roof."

I reach into my pockets and realize they're empty. I pull them out so he can see.

"Where's your driver's license?"

"Back pocket."

"Reach back and pull it out."

I do as he says.

He takes his time, but finally gives it back to me and says, "Does this look like Pee Wee Herman's Fun House to you?"

"No sir."

"What kind of doctor comes to the riverbank to pull his pud?"

"I wasn't—"

"Are there any more of you? Please don't tell me an army of New York doctors has chosen my beloved city to host a circle-jerk!"

"There was a girl."

"A girl? I don't see a girl. Is she in the trunk?"

"No sir."

"You know what I see, Dr. Box?"

"What's that, officer?"

"I see a peter-pumpin' pecker-puller."

"I bet you can't say that five times," I say.

"You better get the fuck outta my town, Doctor. Because if I catch you within five miles of a school yard I'll bring you to room temperature before you can say hard-on!"

He gives me a long look.

"Got it, officer. Sorry."

He shakes his head in disgust and leaves.

I wait five minutes until I'm sure he's gone, then look around for the keys, give up, then head up the hill to find Zander.

Chapter 36

AS YOU MAY have guessed, Zander is nowhere to be found.

I try to call her, but get a recorded voice message.

"Zander!" I say. "Please call me back! I don't blame you for leaving, and I'm not upset about the money. I just need my car keys."

I take my life in my hands by approaching a parked car. "Please don't shoot!" I say, loudly. "I need some help. A young lady's gone missing."

I see a flash of hairy ass and then a guy rolls down the front window and says, "How young?"

"Early twenties."

"Fuck off!"

I go back to the car, call Zander again, get no response.

I face the fact I've been robbed.

It's okay. I've still got my wallet. I've also got another fifteen grand in my medical bag.

I play it in my mind. When she pulled my pants down and rummaged around in her handbag she wasn't looking for a condom.

She'd already emptied my pockets. She was stuffing my cash in her bag.

Why did she take the wine with her?

Who knows? Fingerprints? DNA? Maybe she really likes the wine.

Where did she go?

I think about it.

She probably had it planned in advance with whoever dropped her off at the junk yard. Maybe Chris, from the bowling alley.

Or her real boyfriend.

I sigh.

She left me my wallet. All things considered, that was damn nice of her. She certainly didn't have to do that.

So why did she take my keys?

I think about it a few minutes and come up with this: she had to walk up the hill carrying the handbag. Probably thought I might turn around on my way to pee. If so, I would've seen her. Maybe she was afraid I'd drive up the hill to save her the walk. And maybe I'd catch her climbing into her boyfriend's car, or Chris's truck.

Then I start thinking about the policeman.

It dawns on me he just showed up.

He didn't drive up in a police car, he just walked down the hill and chewed me out. Then he walked back up the hill.

Did he visit any of the other cars?

No.

So either Zander ran into him on the hill and told him I was jerking off in the car...

Or he's the boyfriend.

I think he's the boyfriend.

Because if he really thought I was a pervert, wouldn't he have arrested me?

I get a sudden sinking feeling, remembering how long he had my wallet when I was leaning against the car with my back to him.

He probably copied all my information in a notebook.

Name. Address. Driver's License. Credit cards, including the security codes.

Shit!

Since he didn't take me in, and didn't have a cop car, he's probably not even a cop.

I call the rental car agency in Nashville and report stolen keys.

It takes ten minutes to convince them the car is safely in my possession.

"Why didn't you say so?" the lady says. "We're hooked up to satellite. We can start your car for you. When you get where you're going, call us back and we'll turn it off and lock it. When you're ready to go again, call us and we'll unlock it and start it up for you again."

I'm amazed, but it seems like a lot of trouble to go through.

"Is there an easier way?"

"You could download the key app and do it yourself from your cell phone."

"Why didn't you say that in the first place?"

"The key app costs ninety-nine cents."

I shake my head. Like I'd spend a hundred-fifty a day to rent the car, but wouldn't spend another buck to make it work. "I'll spring for it," I say. "How do I find the app?"

Chapter 37

THE PHONE APP to start the car is amazing. The sort of thing I wish I'd invented. When you bring it up it looks exactly like the remote control that was built into the key. There are four buttons. The top one locks the car. Bottom left unlocks it. Bottom right unlocks the trunk. Center button starts or shuts off the engine. I press the center button, and the engine starts. Like I say, amazing. I put the car in gear and make my way up the riverbank. When I get to the top, I park while deciding what to do next.

I think about driving to Zander's house, but realize I don't know her address. I consider filing a police report, but apart from a wounded ego and the loss of what to me is a small amount of cash, it would be a complete hassle.

There are two women still in the mix: Trudy, who probably doesn't want me now that she's independently wealthy, and Renee Williams, the thirty-year-old kindergarten teacher whose husband ran off with her best friend. Renee being my sure thing.

Given the choice, I'd take Trudy over Renee in a heartbeat. Except that I'm ninety minutes from Starbucks, where Trudy lies in a hospital bed, currently unable to have sex.

I call Renee.

"Hello?"

"Hi Renee, It's Gideon Box, from Manhattan."

"Kansas?"

"New York City."

"Gideon Box?"

"The doctor. We met on the dating site?"

She pauses a beat.

"Omigod!" she squeals. "I'm so *sorry*! You're Dr. Box! Yes, absolutely! Hi! How *are* you?"

"I'm great."

"What's up, Doc?" she says, then laughs hysterically.

"Funny," I say. Then say, "Have you met a handsome, famous movie star yet?"

"Nope."

"How about an airplane pilot?"

She giggles. "Nope."

"In that case, I thought you should know I'm in Kentucky."

"Omigod! *Where?*"

"Have you ever heard of a place called Paducah?"

"Of course, silly! It's not but thirty minutes from here! Can I come see you?"

See *me?* That happy thought hadn't even crossed my mind.

"Yes, of course!" I say. "But I don't have a hotel room yet."

"You won't get one, either. Not in Paducah."

"Why, is there a convention?"

"In Paducah?"

She laughs. "Not that I know of. I just mean there are no *hotels* in Paducah. But they've got some decent motels. How about I jump in the car and head that way? When I get to town I'll call and you can tell me where you are."

"Sounds great. I'll get a room, check in, and wait to hear from you."

"I'm so excited, Gideon!"

"Me, too!"

"By the way," she says, "I *love* your name! Gideon sounds noble, and grand. I'm sorry I didn't remember it. I always think of you as Dr. Box."

"That's quite alright."

"See you soon!"

"Can't wait."

Here's what I know about Renee Williams: she's thirty, she's a kindergarten teacher, her husband ran off with her best friend, and she's looking for revenge. According to Renee, the best revenge would be to have an affair with her best friend's husband.

If her best friend's husband was successful.

Or even good-looking.

Or even clean.

Since he's none of those things, her first choice is a handsome, famous movie star, an airplane pilot, or a rich doctor.

She didn't say a young, good-looking doctor.

She said a rich one.

Like I said, Renee Williams is a sure thing.

Chapter 38

RENEE WAS WRONG. Paducah actually does have a hotel, and it's a famous one. But I want to be in a newer area, near the interstate, so I found a surprisingly decent, clean, king suite with a kitchen, desk, couch and all the amenities you could hope to get for a hundred thirty-five a night. I'm not trying to impress you with the room. It's not *that* nice. Even in New York City it wouldn't run more than two-twenty.

But in New York City it wouldn't be this clean.

I call Renee to tell her I'm staying at the Royal Landmark Inn, and she says, "Wow! Perfect timing!"

"You can't already *be* here," I say.

"No, silly!" she says. "I'm still at home getting all pretty for you. But I'm standing here in tub water, naked, with a razor in my hand."

I wonder if she's contemplating suicide. Surely she can wait till after our date for that.

She says, "How do you like it?"

"Like what?"

"Are you going to make me say it?"

"Yes." Because I have no idea what she's talking about.

"Oh, so you like *dirty* talk?"

I now have even less idea what she's talking about.

But I do like dirty talk when a naked woman's on top, bitch-slapping me with her tits. Or yelling at me as I hammer her from behind when she's face-down, ass-up, on her knees. In contrast, I didn't care for the dirty talk I got from Zander's fake-cop boyfriend a few minutes ago. If Renee is anything like her photos, she's nothing like Zander's boyfriend. So I'm probably on safe ground by saying, "I *love* dirty talk!"

"Oooh, I bet you do-oo-oooh," she says with what she considers a sexy voice. "Well, aren't *you* a bad doctor boy! You *are* a bad doctor, aren't you?"

"Yes."

Renee's got me pegged. I may be a great surgeon, but I *am* a bad doctor. I hear it all the time. I've got a terrible bedside manner, and have problems communicating with people. Half the time I have no idea what they're even talking about.

Like now.

She says, "Oh, bad boy?"

"Yes?"

"Don't forget, I'm standing here, completely naked."

"Wow!"

"Mmmm! And you know what I'm doing?"

"What?"

"I'm looking at my pussy."

"Wow!"

"Would you like to see it?"

"Absolutely!"

"Try to picture it right now."

"Okay."

"Do you see where I'm going with this? I'm trying to decide how you like it."

I get it.

She's role-playing.

I say, "Doggie-style!"

She pauses a few seconds, then laughs. "I guess that means full bush. Well, you surprised me, but no problem. I'll just be there that much sooner! Should I pack an overnight bag?"

Seriously? She plans to stay after having sex with me? And does that mean there could be an encore? Or morning sex?

I can't remember the last time I had morning sex.

You know, *sober* morning sex.

I like it.

On the other hand, do I really want a total stranger spending the night in my room?

It's one thing to fuck a total stranger. Quite another to trust her while you're sleeping.

What if Renee turns out to be the love child of *Hell Bitch* and *Night of the Living Dead*?

"Bring the overnight bag and we'll see how things develop," I say, realizing I have plenty of time to work out my trust issues before giving my final answer.

She hangs up.

What was it she said? Full bush?

What the hell did *that* mean?

She had a razor in her hand. Wondered how I like it. And I said doggie style, and she said full bush, and...

Ah! I get it.

Shit.

I might be fucking Wolfman Jack tonight.

Chapter 39

I'VE GOT FORTY minutes to kill while waiting for Renee to show up. If I were an author, writing a book, instead of a guy telling you a story, I'd fill the next ten pages telling you how this area was originally a Chickasaw village, and how Chief Paduke welcomed the settlers and lived in harmony till 1827, when William Clark, of Lewis and Clark, showed up with a phony five dollar land deed and forced the Indians to move to Mississippi. I'd tell you that after building the town, Clark was brazen enough to invite Chief Paduke to the ribbon-cutting ceremony, and that the Chief showed up, but died of malaria on the way home.

To impress you with my research I might mention Paducah is one of two cities mentioned in the song, *Hooray for Hollywood.*

But do you really care?

I don't think so.

My guess is you'd rather hear about Renee Williams.

Here's my take on the kindergarten teacher: she's medium cute. I realize that statement requires clarification, and I'm not sure I'm up to it, but I'll try.

You know how a puppy's adorable when he's sleeping or playing but a grown dog's disgusting when he humps your leg or licks his dick?

Renee's the opposite.

Meaning, she's not the least bit adorable, but I like the way she humps me and licks my dick. I like it so much I hardly look up when the door flies open and Zander's fake cop boyfriend enters the room with two other guys dressed as policemen.

What gets our attention is all three are holding guns on us.

Chapter 40

TURNS OUT ZANDER'S boyfriend is a real cop. Also, he's not Zander's boyfriend.

Turns out the reason he didn't arrest me at the riverbank is because I hadn't exposed myself, and he's experienced enough to know a good attorney could reasonably argue I parked there to take a nap and was simply scratching an itch when he happened by.

Turns out the reason he didn't drive his car down the riverbank is because his partner was busy flirting with the cute young lady with the big handbag (Zander) who said there was a creepy guy in a rental car down the hill, pleasuring himself (me).

Then a car pulled up, Zander climbed in, and they drove away.

No, they didn't have any reason to question the driver or record the license plate.

I learned the nicest way possible that Renee trimmed her orange bush in the shape of a heart for my benefit, and didn't appreciate the attention it received from the policemen, particularly the one whose son attended her kindergarten class at Logan Elementary.

The good news is, they allow Renee to go free after being convinced she had nothing to do with the armed robbery that took place at the bowling alley earlier in the day. The one where a female employee named Chris wrote down the make, model, and license number of the rental car she saw in the employee's parking lot.

After giving police a detailed description of me.

Chapter 41

THIS IS EMBARRASSING.

I'm in a police lineup with two black guys, an old wino who's pissing his pants as we speak, and a cross-dressing punk rocker who shit in hers long before I got here.

Guess which of us was eye-witnessed driving the rental car?

Me.

No surprise there.

But there is a surprise.

A big one.

Chris, a.k.a. Zander's "friend", fingers me as the guy who, acting alone, forced his way into the bowling alley, put a gun to her head, and made her open the owner's private safe.

The cops aren't overly impressed with my story, that Zander scheduled a date with me in order to dupe me into being the getaway driver for her robbery.

Can you blame them?

So they book me and it appears I'll be spending the night at city jail.

But when my background check comes back and Paducah police learn I'm the world's greatest cardio-thoracic surgeon, a guy who earns two hundred grand per operation, my story suddenly sounds better than Chris's.

After an hour of rigorous interrogation, Chris admits Zander set the whole thing up and gave her half the money.

Chris's boyfriend picked Zander up from the riverbank, accepted Chris's half of the money for her, and drove Zander to a truck stop in Eddyville, Kentucky. When he dropped her off, he called Chris's cellphone, and Chris reported the robbery.

Nearly two hours after it took place.

What made Chris finally spill her guts?

Outrage.

Zander gave Chris and her boyfriend half the bowling alley money, as promised.

But when Chris heard about the eight-thousand dollar robbery that took place around my ankles at the riverbank, she freaked out. She felt half of that should have gone into her pocket.

Police can't locate anyone named Zander Evans in their data banks. The detectives can't even get a hit on Google.

I tell them about the dating website, but they tell me she's pulled her photo and closed her account. It could take the police department weeks to gain access to the original records.

They're happy to hear I've got recent photos of Zander on my cell phone.

They download the photos, take down my information, and tell me I'll need to come back to town at some point to testify against Zander and/or Chris.

I tell the cop who's not Zander's boyfriend I'm willing to come back if I can fit it into my schedule.

"I could jail you till then, if that would make things easier for you," he says.

I hope they never catch Zander.

Not because she has my support, but because if I have to testify against her the entire riverbank episode will be on the public record. Can you imagine how embarrassing it would be for me if the multi-million dollar donors to my hospital found out their top surgeon was unable to sustain an erection during a routine blowjob?

It's late by the time I get back to the hotel, and I'm exhausted. But not too exhausted to open the door for Renee, who wants to spend the night despite the unwelcome police visit earlier.

"What made you decide to come back?" I say.

"You know that cop whose son was in my class at school last semester?"

"Yeah?"

"I figure it won't matter so much that he saw me naked if you and I wind up getting married," she says, hopefully.

"That's quite true," I say, shamelessly.

"There's been a slight change since I saw you," she says. "I went to McDonalds to get one of their dollar meals, you know?"

No. I don't, but I say, "What happened?"

"I had to use the bathroom."

"And?"

"I got my period, is all. That's not a problem for you, is it? I mean, being a doctor and all?"

"Depends on how you feel."

"About doing it?"

"I mean, do you feel up to having sex?"

"Yes, of course!" she says. "I'm not one to let it slow *me* down!"

"Well, that's a damn fine piece of news," I say, and mean it.

"So it's not a problem?"

"Not for me."

"You know what really feels good this time of the month?" she says.

"What's that?"

"Oral sex."

"I know. You showed me. And you know what?"

"What?"

"You're damned good at it!"

"Really?"

"Really. You want to have another go?"

"Thanks, Gideon. That's really sweet of you. But I meant me."

"What about you?"

"It feels extra good to me when...you know."

"Whoa. You want *me* to give *you* oral?"

"Yes."

"Seriously?"

"A *real* man would!" she says.

I look at my watch. "You know what I just realized?" I say.

"What's that?"

"I haven't had dinner yet. Are you hungry?"

"Well, I *did* eat from the dollar menu a little while ago."

"Oh."

"You know what we could do? Order you some room service. And while we're waiting for your dinner to arrive, maybe we could...you know."

I order us two bottles of wine and pray they arrive before she gets naked.

Chapter 42

AFTER ORDERING THE wine I turn to see Renee lying on the bed, naked from the waist down. She says, "Come and get it, Cowboy!"

Using the excuse of needing a shower before getting intimate, I lock myself in the bathroom, turn on the shower, and text the following message to my hospital administrator, Bruce Luce:

I need a big favor! Flood my cell phone with text messages, telling me I have to fly to NYC immediately to perform a life-saving surgery.

I press send. When it goes through, I type another:

Text me you've got a jet waiting at the private landing strip in Paducah, and tell me it's a matter of life and death!

When that one goes through I send him another:

The messages need to sound extremely urgent! Start sending them immediately! And don't stop sending them till I tell you.

When that one goes through, I erase all the sent messages from my phone, and open the bathroom door.

"You're awfully dry for having just taken a shower!" Renee says. "Plus, the water's still running."

"I was brushing my teeth," I say, "then realized I had my phone with me. I get emergency calls all the time. A kid nearly died once when I was in the shower and couldn't hear the phone."

"That's *terrible!*" she says.

"Can you keep an eye on my phone while I shower, just in case?"

"I'd *love* to!" she says. "And by the way, don't worry about going hungry. I called room service back and ordered you a Porterhouse steak and a baked potato with butter, sour cream, and bacon bits."

"You did?"

"And some blackberry cobbler."

"That's a significant caloric commitment."

She laughs. "I hope you don't plan to talk like that when we order food in Logan."

"What would happen?"

"They'd probably take you out back and shoot you."

"That's a tough restaurant."

"By the way, the room service guy said your order will take forty minutes. That sounds about right, don't you think?"

She winks, pats her heart-shaped muff.

"Sounds great!" I say, feigning enthusiasm.

I put my phone on the night stand beside her.

"Let me know if anyone calls, okay?"

"I promise."

"Texts are particularly serious."

"Texts are? How come?"

"It means the people in charge are knee-deep in a critical situation, and there's no time to talk."

"Wow!"

"I can't express how important this is, Renee. I'm counting on you."

"I won't let you down," she says, solemnly. "I'll let you know if anyone calls or texts. I promise."

"Good girl. Thank you."

"You're very welcome. I love the fact you save children's lives."

"Really?"

"Of course. I'm a kindergarten teacher, remember?"

"Right."

"You work on their bodies, I work on their minds."

"I like that," I say, truthfully.

It strikes me Renee's a good person. While that's a plus, it's not enough to make me want to dive face first into Red River Gorge.

I strip, enter the shower, but leave the door unlocked.

A minute later, I hear her call out my name in an urgent manner.

I smile, pretending not to hear.

The door opens.

"Gideon!" she says.

I poke my head out of the shower. "Everything okay?"

She's holding my cell phone, pointing to it. There's a look of panic in her eyes.

"I got a text?"

She nods.

"Read it to me."

"There are two messages."

"Don't tell me it's Bruce Luce."

"Would that be bad?"

"*Terribly* bad! Don't tell me Bruce sent me two texts!"

"One's from Bruce."

"Just one?"

"Uh huh."

"Still, that's got to be really bad."

"It is. I'm so sorry!"

I suppress a smile. "Read it to me."

"The one from Bruce?"

"Yes, of course!"

"It says, 'Fuck you, Gideon!'"

"*What?*"

"I'm sorry," she says.

I hate Bruce Luce. Now what am I going to do?

"Who sent the other text?" I ask.

"I don't know."

"Read it."

She reads it, but not out loud. As she does, her face undergoes a major transformation. Like a cartoon character, her cheeks turn red, her eyes become slits, and steam seems to escape from her ears.

"I don't fucking believe it!" she says.

"What?"

She frowns deeply and glares at me.

"Who's it from?" I ask.

"Trudy Lake."

I turn off the water. "Trudy Lake?"

Her face is smoldering. This is not a happy teacher.

"You actually know someone named Trudy Lake?" I say.

"It appears we both do," she says between clenched teeth.

"I wonder how many Trudy Lakes there must be in the world?" I say.

"How many would *you* guess, Gideon?"

"Thousands."

"With a 270 area code?"

"How do you know Trudy?" I say.

She stares me down and says, "You first."

"What did she write?"

"'Call me.' Then she gave you her number."

"Trudy Lake?"

"Yeah, that's right, Slick."

Based on nothing more than her steely-eyed glare, I'm guessing Renee's not a Trudy Lake fan. That makes sense. I picture the map of Western Kentucky in my mind and realize the two women live less than an hour apart. This area's filled with small towns. Everyone knows everyone. Trudy was the homecoming queen, the prettiest, most popular girl in the county. She's bound to have female enemies, girls who lost out to her in beauty pageants, cheerleader tryouts, homecoming courts. But Renee's not pretty enough to have been involved in those activities. Plus, she's twelve years older than Trudy. So I wonder about the connection.

There's no denying she's royally pissed.

I decide to keep it casual, saying, "I met Trudy last night at a restaurant in Clayton. She was my waitress. I'm sure I gave her a bigger tip than she usually gets."

Noting the fireworks in Renee's eyes, I add, "As I would for any waitress who doesn't screw up my order."

"Why was she texting you?"

"I have no idea. Maybe she wanted to thank me for the tip."

"How'd she get your phone number?"

"Um..."

"Yeah?"

I'm standing in the shower, naked. She's got me cornered. There's no place to run, no place to hide, no way to escape.

I ask, "How is it you know Trudy?"

"She's my sister."

Chapter 43

IF YOU EVER want to see a woman at her angriest, fuck her sister.

Renee's punching and slapping at me and trying to bite me. I'm doing my best to keep the shower curtain between us, while wondering if the state's motto should be *Welcome to Kentucky: three million people, twelve last names!*

I remember Trudy said Scooter was a lot older than her mom, and had started another family before they met. I had no way of knowing Renee was related to Trudy, but I'm willing to fuck my way through the entire family to get to Trudy, if that's what it takes.

Renee pulls the shower rod down and starts flailing away at me while explaining she's always had to play second fiddle to Trudy. Precious Trudy, the young, pretty half-sister. The one her father chose to live with. The homecoming queen with the four-point-oh grade point average and sparkling personality.

"I can't believe you *fucked my sister!*" she yells as she pounds me into a fetal position.

Somewhere between the slaps, punches, and tears—hers, not mine—I manage to calm her down enough to say I never had sex with her sister.

"*Swear it!*" she yells.

"I swear."

"You did exactly what to her?"

"I might have kissed her."

"*Kissed* her?"

"I might have. You know, like a peck on the cheek?"

"That's it?"

"Yes."

"She didn't handcuff you to the fence and suck your dick?"

"*What?*"

"She's been known to do that."

"*What?*"

Now *I'm* pissed.

Chapter 44

Trudy Lake.

DR. BOX BEAT me up pretty good last night. My eyes are so swollen I can barely see out of them. If I shift in my hospital bed the slightest bit it hurts. And a while ago I peed blood. The good news is everyone bought it. Our story, I mean. Not my pee.

Even Darrell thinks he's the one that did this to me, which is a fair indicator of how fucked up on drugs he was last night. He sent word to me through one of the nurses.

He's sorry.

"How badly hurt is he?" I ask.

"Well, he lost his spleen."

"Is that important?"

"It helps with the immune system, but you don't need it to live."

"Well, that's good news."

The nurse shakes her head and chuckles.

"What?"

"That Darrell. He's a funny one."

"Funny?"

"He asked if we could save his spleen and give it back to him when he checks out."

"Why?"

"The doctor said it was the biggest one he's ever seen."

"Knowin' Darrell, he's proud to have the biggest anythin'."

"He says he's got a taxidermist friend who can mount it, and he'd like to hang it in the bedroom, right above the bed. He said, 'Trudy might like that.'"

She laughs at the thought and says, "Can you just imagine?"

I say, "Well of course I can! I've known him four years! And in Darrell's brain, why wouldn't that be comfortin'? Bein' able to look up at my husband's spleen every mornin' when I open my eyes, knowing it was watchin' over us the night before?"

They both laugh.

"Is it true he's your husband and your brother?"

"Half brother. And I'd rather not talk about it."

"Reason I asked, after my mom passed, my fifteen-year-old sister married our stepfather."

"Oh, my God!" I say. "That had to be weird."

"Weirder than you think. I was seventeen at the time and had to live with them for two years, since I couldn't afford a place of my own. Want to hear the best part?"

"Of course!"

"Until I turned eighteen, social services classified my younger sister as my custodial mother!"

I laugh, hard, despite the pain. Then say, "I'm so sorry. I don't mean to laugh."

"That's okay. I'm laughing too. I was just letting you know I've been there."

"Oh, I almost forgot. Thanks for chargin' up my phone this afternoon while I napped."

"Well, I keep a charger here just for that purpose."

"It was real nice of you."

I let her do her job a few minutes, then ask, "Besides his spleen, will Darrell mend?"

"He will, but he'll walk funny for a long time. I don't envy his P.T."

"What's that?"

"Physical therapy. It'll be a long, painful process, recovering the use of his legs."

"But he will?"

"Eventually. He won't be like he was, but he'll be able to get around."

"I don't take comfort in Darrell's sufferin'," I say. "But I don't feel sorry for him, either. He's been a bullyin' force in my life for too long. Dr. Box did the right thing."

The nurse nods, and says, "Darrell will want to know if you have any messages for him."

"Tell him I'm sorry he lost his spleen," I say.

When I'm lucid enough to function normally, I check my messages and see where Gideon tried to call me a couple of times earlier today. I want to talk to him and thank him for the incredibly generous gift, but I've been busy with one visitor after another for the past two hours, and of course, policeman Clem's been in my room most of the time. Whenever we find ourselves alone he tries to talk me into a courtship.

Gawd.

I don't want to talk to Dr. Box with Clem in the room, nor do I know if he's available to talk right now. So I text him a simple, two-word message: *Call Me!* And type in my cell number. If he calls, I'll ask Clem to give me some privacy, and maybe Dr. Box and I can sort out our true feelin's.

My guess is Dr. Box wants me back. He was headed to Ralston to visit Faith Hemphill, a woman he met on a datin' site, but that didn't work out. Their date got cut short when two burglars broke into Faith's house and shot each other before Dr. Box turned up.

Don't ask me how two burglars can shoot each other to death while tryin' to rob an unarmed widow, but that's how it went down, accordin' to Sheriff Boyd, who spoke to the Ralston police. Of course, when I heard the burglars were Cletus and Renfro, it all came together.

Cletus and Renfro were Darrell's meth cookers. While I don't like to speak ill of the newly departed, it's no secret that mentally speakin', their driveways didn't quite reach the road.

Darrell, whose own mental antenna can't pick up the premium channels, obviously told them to drive to Faith's house and kill Dr. Box. Darrell's widely known for his jealousy, which makes me partly to blame for the twins' death and Dr. Box's busted date. What I mean to say is "broken date," since I don't know if Faith is busty or not.

But speakin' of Faith, you might be wonderin' how Darrell knew who she was and where she lived. Those are good questions, and here's another: how did Darrell know Dr. Box was headin' to her place for a date?

Only one way I can think of.

Daddy.

Sheriff Boyd must've questioned Dr. Box, and shared the information with Daddy. And why wouldn't he? Him and Daddy have been thicker than thieves since before I can remember. If he told Daddy about Faith Hemphill, you know he told Daddy about the hand job. It's embarrassin' enough Clem knows about it. Can't wait to hear Daddy's take on it.

So Sheriff Boyd told Daddy about Faith, and Daddy told Darrell, hopin' he'd tell Cletus and Renfro to kill Dr. Box.

Why?

Best I can tell, Daddy benefits from Dr. Box's death two ways. First, it keeps him out of my pants. Dr. Box, I mean, not Daddy. Second, it prevents Dr. Box from testifyin' against Daddy in court for attempted murder.

Hang on a sec, I'm getting a text.

This is weird.

It's from my half-sister, Renee Williams. It says: *Keep your ass away from Dr. Gideon Box! I won't tell you again!*

What?

Oh, my!

Poor Gideon.

If he's hooked up with Renee he's in for wild ride.

What circumstances could possibly come together to cause the two of them to run into each other? I wonder where they met, and which story she's told. She usually poses as a fundraiser for an organization that helps grant memorable experiences for dyin' children, but sometimes she pretends to be a librarian, kindergarten teacher, undercover cop, or fishing guide.

Fishing guide's the worst. If Renee takes you out on her bass boat, you're likely to stay wet a long time, since fishing lures don't run deep enough to snag clothin' where she claims to sink her bodies.

That's a terribly unfair statement for me to make, since it's based totally on rumors and a recording of drunk talk from Renee herself taped by a shiftless Tennessee reporter who misrepresented himself as a suitor and got her plastered one night, hopin' to break the story of what become of Renee's husband and best friend.

That was nearly two years ago, and while the rumors and drunken statements were inadmissible, they were deemed credible enough to cause officials to devote two weeks to draggin' the lower part of Kentucky Lake for the bodies. Of course, it was wasted effort, since the lake's a hundred and eighty-four miles long, up to two miles wide, and three hundred-sixty feet deep. Not to mention Renee could have cut through the pass to Lake Barkley to sink the bodies. That lake is almost as long, wide, and deep.

Being that Renee's family, I try extra hard not to judge her.

But others have.

The only reason she's on this side of prison bars is the lack of bodies and two barely-hung juries. Both juries polled guilty, eleven to one. But eleven ain't twelve, and the small Tennessee county where she was livin' didn't have the funds to try her a third time.

Renee bounced back, wound up marryin' her jailer, Roy Williams, got a teachin' certificate, and seemed to be headin' in the right direction with her life. But Roy suffered a stroke and lost his job, and Renee divorced him, moved to Logan County, and got a job teaching kindergarten that came to an end a few weeks ago when her past caught up to her.

"Somethin' wrong, Trudy?" Clem says, from his post at the back of the room.

"Nope, I'm fine."

"Want me to re-arrange your pillows again?"

"Nope, I'm good. Thanks."

Dr. Box arranged for me to receive ten thousand dollars a month for the next two years. While it's much more than I need, it's an insanely generous gift. It wouldn't be right to accept that much money.

But I'll accept some.

Enough to get me started with a new life.

My relationship with Dr. Box seemed to end before it got started. I was hopin' for more, but I think my family history scared him off.

As it should have.

I'd been prepared to step aside and let him go on with his life, but that was before I realized how much he needs me. And he does, at least for the near future.

Dr. Box is in serious danger, and I need to warn him.

What concerns me most?

Renee texted me from his cell phone.

I can't think of any scenario in which Dr. Box would willingly allow my crazy sister to screen his messages or text people from his phone.

Especially me.

I know he wants to talk to me, or he wouldn't have called me twice this afternoon.

I shake my head, thinkin' about the rough twenty-four hours my family's put Dr. Box through. First, Daddy knocked him unconscious. Then he robbed him, kicked his nuts, and hung him. Then the barn roof collapsed on him. Then he lost a possible love connection with Faith, when the people my brother and husband Darrell sent to kill him shot each other instead. And now my sister Renee is likely holdin' him against his will, and makin' threats against me that'll eventually drive her to punish him.

If I can somehow manage to protect Dr. Box from Renee, Daddy, Darrell, and the local police, and if he and I wind up gettin' engaged someday, can you just imagine the scene my kinfolk will make at our weddin'?

Chapter 45

"CLEM, COULD YOU give me a few minutes of privacy?" I say.

"You're not gonna call *him*, are you?"

"That's none of your business."

He frowns. "I don't like it. And I sure as hell don't like *him*."

Great.

Dr. Box has managed to make yet another enemy in law enforcement.

When Clem leaves the room I call Dr. Box, but get no answer.

"Clem!" I shout.

He comes flyin' through the door.

"What's wrong?"

"Call Sheriff Boyd."

"Why?"

"I need to talk to him."

"What about?"

"Just call him."

"He's gonna ask why."

"Maybe so, but he'll come."

He glares at me a minute, and I glare back.

"I don't like it," he says.

"Why am I not surprised?"

Chapter 46

Dr. Gideon Box.

I'VE GONE THROUGH a lot of emotions over the past twenty-four hours. Heard good things, weird things, bad things. Learning I was about to be hung was the worst, hands down. I mean, literally, my hands were down, cuffed behind my back. So that was the worst.

A close second was learning I'm not the first guy Trudy's fence-kissed.

Worse, according to her own sister, Trudy's blown other guys at the very same fence.

And here I thought I was special.

I come out of the shower, dejected.

Renee sees it. She can tell my mood has shifted.

"I'm here for you, Gideon," she says.

I grab my clothes from the sink as I pass her, heading to the bed. I sit, put my socks on, then stand and finish dressing.

"Can I ask you a question?" she asks.

I raise a palm. "Why not?"

"What happened to your neck?"

Something in the way she asked the question makes me do a double-take.

I can't explain how, but I do believe Renee knows her Daddy had something to do with the rope burn around my neck.

"You just noticed that?" I say.

"Of course not! I noticed it right off. I think you might have a permanent mark there."

Now I have two lovely thoughts. The woman I love gives blowjobs at the dumpster, and her father gives permanent rope-burn tattoos.

There's a knock at the door.

"Room service!" a voice calls out from the hall.

I notice Renee's still naked from the waist down.

She backs into the bathroom and closes the door. I let him in, he sets up the food, and leaves. When Renee comes out I can tell she's been crying.

"What's wrong?"

"This is all going badly," she says.

"What is?"

"Our date."

I nod.

"It's all because of *her*!" she says.

"Who?"

"Trudy."

She's right. But I say, "That's not true. It's just that I had a horrible time at the police station earlier."

"Oh my God!" she says. "You're right! I was so excited to see you, I never asked what happened!"

I wave her off.

"It's not that big a deal."

"Of course it is! You were a suspect in an armed robbery! I can't believe I never asked about your experience. I'm a *horrible* girlfriend. Truly horrible!"

"Don't be silly."

"Here's what we're going to do," she says, walking around the bed. "You've got a fine dinner here. We'll sit together, have some wine. You'll tell me all about your afternoon at the police station, while enjoying your meal."

She leans down, lifts her purse from the floor, places it on the bed in front of her.

I say, "Can I be honest, Renee?"

"Of course, darling."

"You're a sweet girl, and the last thing I want to do is offend you."

"But?"

"I'm afraid I've lost my appetite."

She smiles. "Nonsense! You haven't eaten all afternoon, you said so yourself. We're going to have a nice quiet evening and you're going to relax and enjoy your dinner."

"No, I'm sorry. I'm just not in the mood."

She pulls a gun from her purse, points it at me, then cocks it.

"I insist," she says.

Chapter 47

HAVE YOU EVER tried to eat dinner with a loaded gun pointed at your face? If so, was the person holding the gun chugging a bottle of wine? And if so, did you enjoy your meal? Reason I ask, I'm having trouble concentrating on the food.

"My Daddy gave you that rope burn, didn't he?" she says.

I nod.

"How'd you escape?"

"It's a long story."

"I'd love to hear it."

"Can I tell you later?"

"Sure. Want to tell me about the police station first?"

"Maybe after dinner."

"Okay," she says, cheerfully.

"Would you consider putting the gun down?"

"Not really. Not yet."

"When?"

"Well," she says, "you were quite the eager beaver till the cops barged in. I thought we really had it going, sex-wise. I mean, you yelled a lot, and carried on like it meant something. But now you seem to have lost interest. I'm trying not to take it personally, but I don't deal well with rejection."

"If you're not planning to get to the point, can you just go ahead and shoot me?"

She smiles. "I like you."

"Don't base too much on a first impression," I say.

"You're a saucy one, Dr. Box!"

I shrug.

The room phone rings.

"I should get that," I say.

"I don't think so."

She lets it ring. Then picks up the phone, calls the front desk, tells them not to put any calls through. She hangs up the phone and says, "You know what I think?"

"I have no idea."

She says, "I think I may have given it up too quickly. The sex, I mean."

"Really?" I say. "Because it seems to me you held out nearly two minutes before taking your clothes off."

"I don't remember you complaining about that. And anyway, we had a history on the internet that gave me reason to believe you might be special. I haven't given up that thought, by the way. But I'm afraid you don't respect me like you should."

"Why's that?"

"You think I'm easy. A tramp...A slut...A whore...Feel free to interrupt me at any time."

"You're doing fine."

She shakes her head and curls her lips into a strange smile and looks at me the way a giant snake might look at a wounded mouse. "I like saucy men," she says. "But you know what?"

"What?"

"I can be saucy, too."

"Oh, joy."

"You know what your problem is?" she says.

"You?"

"No. Your problem is we haven't spent any quality time together. As friends."

"Is this how you treat your friends? By holding a gun on them?"

"Sometimes."

"Do you reciprocate?"

"What do you mean?"

"Ever let your friends hold the gun on *you*?"

She smiles. "I like the way you word things. You've got a fine mind, Gideon. Ever thought about being a kindergarten teacher?"

"Every hour of every day."

She laughs heartily. When it dies down she says, "Here's what we're going to do."

"Tell me."

"When you finish eating, we're going to do what normal couples do."

"What's that?"

She fumbles around in her purse with one hand while holding the gun on me with the other. Eventually, she finds what she's looking for, and places it on the table between us.

A bottle of nail polish.

"I don't understand," I say.

"You're going to paint my toenails," she says.

"You're joking."

"When we do good deeds for others, we feel good about ourselves."

"We do?"

"It builds our self-esteem. And helps us flex our empathy muscles. It's the first step toward being good neighbors. And you know what that helps you become?"

"Crazy?"

"A citizen of the world."

"All this from painting your toenails? Who knew? We should call the United Nations immediately. Can peace be far behind?"

"Go ahead," she says. "Make jokes."

"What's the point? You'll only laugh."

She laughs.

"See?"

She says. "I really do like you, Gideon. I can see why Trudy wants you. But that will never happen."

"Why not?"

"She's too young and pretty for you. And doesn't know how to please a man."

Renee's way off base about Trudy's ability to please a man. I think about the hand job in the car until I see Renee staring at my face.

"Something wrong?" I say.

"Looks like you were daydreaming about something pleasant. I mention Trudy, you get a goofy smile on your face. We're going to have to work on that."

"How?"

"By adjusting your focus. From her to me."

"And you think painting your nails will accomplish that?"

"Yes. Because painting my nails is something you can do *for* me, to show you value me as a person. And when we show others we value them, we open ourselves up to wonderful possibilities. Like friendship. Is that something you'd be willing to do?"

"I'd be willing to cut off my ears if it would make you stop using that stupid kindergarten voice."

She frowns.

I say, "You seriously believe by forcing me to paint your nails I'll become a better person?"

"Yes. And you'll do other things to show you value me not only as a person, but as a life partner."

My turn to frown. "Life partner?"

"Of course 'life' is a relative term. While I can guarantee we'll be partners for life, it's up to you how long our partnership will last."

"Because it ends with my death?"

"Yes, of course."

"What else will you force me to do?"

"To help you value me as a person?"

"Yeah. Whatever."

"After the nail ceremony, I'll allow you to please me orally, like we discussed earlier. I'll give you detailed instructions until you master the perfect combination that causes my bud to bloom. After you satisfy my needs, we'll go in the bathroom, and I'll make a nice doo doo in the potty. Then I'll let you wipe my behind. You're making a strange face. What's on your mind, darling?"

"The many ways I'm going to torture my therapist before killing her."

"You're making a joke."

"*You* are, if you think I'm going to wipe your ass."

"Wiping my behind seems gross to you?"

"Shockingly, yes."

She smiles. "That's because you don't see it for what it is."

"Please enlighten me. What is it?"

"A display of nurturing love. Which as we all know, is the precursor to true, eternal love."

"Maybe that explains why I've never been in love."

"Gideon?"

"What?"

"If something happened to you tomorrow, I'd nurture and care for you the rest of your life. I know it sounds unpleasant, cleaning a grownup's potty pants, but it's not gross when you're taking care of the person you love."

"Please tell me you're aware we never laid eyes on each other before this afternoon."

"We're soul mates, Gideon. We've traveled this road many times, through many lives."

"I don't think so."

"No?"

"I'm pretty sure I'd remember wiping your ass from one life to the next."

"Don't be impudent, Gideon. Finish your dinner. You'll need your strength for later."

Chapter 48

Trudy Lake.

"YOUR BOYFRIEND CERTAINLY gets around," Sheriff Boyd says. "I'll give him that much. So how do you know he's in Paducah?"

"While waiting for you to show up this past *hour*," I say with no small amount of anger, "I called half the motels within a fifty mile radius of Logan, where Renee lives."

"And you finally found him checked into the Royal Landmark Inn?"

"Yes. Can you call the Paducah police department and have them check on him?"

"Why don't you just call Dr. Box at the Inn and ask if he's okay?"

"You think I haven't tried?"

"No answer?"

"No. But the last five times I've called, they said Dr. Box has asked not to be disturbed."

"Maybe they're having sex. Maybe you're jealous to learn your sister's fucking your boyfriend."

From behind us, Clem laughs.

"Shut up, Clem!" I holler. "Sheriff, this is Renee Williams we're talking about. She kills people."

"Not according to the laws of the state of Tennessee, she doesn't."

"She's taken over his phone. She threatened me."

"Is that the only message she sent? To keep your ass away from Doctor Box? And she won't tell you again? Because that's not much of a threat, Trudy. If it was, I'd be arresting every pre-pubescent girl in junior high. And I hope you know I can't go around banging on hotel doors demanding grown men and women tell me what they're up to."

"You're refusing to help me?"

"If by 'help' you mean will I chase down your boyfriend and make him stop dating your sister, the answer is no."

"How will you feel if Dr. Box turns up dead?"

"Honestly? I'll feel relieved."

"Then go fuck yourself."

"That's an awfully ugly sentence to come from such a pretty face. I expect your mom would be ashamed of what's become of her sweet daughter."

"My mom would be proud of me for tryin' to save a man's life."

"I guess we already found out how proud of you she was."

I try to slap him, but he backs out of the way and says, "You have a nice day now, Mrs. Lake, you hear?"

Chapter 49

I'M DOUBLY SHOCKED when Detective Tan from the Paducah police department takes my call. Shocked he took my call, even more shocked when he said, "We arrested Dr. Box earlier today for armed robbery."

"That's *insane!*" I say.

"Yes, ma'am, we agree. Turns out he was set up by a woman."

"Renee Williams."

"Uh...no ma'am."

"Excuse me?"

"Zander Evans, of Paducah, aged twenty-two, last seen at Mason's Truck Stop, Eddyville, Kentucky. That was four hours ago, give or take. You don't happen to know Miss Evans, do you?"

"No. But I happen to know Dr. Box was in the company of my sister, quite recently."

"And her name?"

"Like I said, Renee Williams."

"Name sounds familiar. Hang on a minute."

When he comes back on he says, "You say Renee Williams is your sister?"

"Yes sir. And she sent me a threatening text from Dr. Box's cell phone. You should know that Renee has been tried two times for a double homicide that occurred in the state of Tennessee a couple years ago, and I have every reason to believe she has ill intentions toward Dr. Box."

"Well, ma'am, I don't normally give out personal information, but I can assure you Dr. Box is not in any danger from Renee Williams."

"How can you say that?"

"Because they're clearly a couple."

"I know it might appear that way, but—"

"Trust me, Mrs. Lake. They're a couple. In every sense of the word."

"Please, Detective, just hear me out. You mentioned another woman."

"Yes ma'am. Zander Evans."

"I happen to know Dr. Box met a woman named Faith Hemphill this morning, in Ralston. How could he possibly have time to see Faith, drive to Paducah, get framed by Zander Evans for a robbery, taken to the station and booked, and set free, and also be involved with Renee Williams?"

"Ma'am, all I'm willing to say is your Dr. Box was having explicit carnal knowledge of your sister at the time of his arrest. And he admitted attempting to engage in carnal relations with Zander Evans less than two hours earlier. I don't know what kind of feed he's on, but this Dr. Box gets more action than a two-peckered rabbit."

"Listen to me, Detective. Dr. Box is in danger. Renee's holdin' him at the Royal Landmark Inn. Maybe they were havin' sex when you arrested them, and maybe they were gettin' along just fine. But sometime after that, she found out he was interested in me, and that's when she sent me a threatenin' message."

"What time was that, ma'am."

"About eight-thirty this evenin'."

"That'd be about forty minutes after we turned him loose."

"Can you please just go there and check on him?"

He sighs. "I'll phone it in."

"Thank you! Will you call me back?"

"I will. But if this is just you, trying to get back at your sister for stealing your boyfriend—"

"It's not. And he's not my boyfriend. He's a mongrel dog who'd fuck a pile of rocks hopin' to find a snake. But his life's in danger, and I won't feel better till you've checked on him. If he's fine and happy bein' with my sister, more power to him. My only intent is to make sure he's safe."

"Can I ask why?"

"He's been very generous to me. I owe him."

"Can you give me a little more to go on?"

"My husband beat me half to death last night. Dr. Box saved my life."

The detective pauses. Then says, "Did your beating have anything to do with Dr. Box?"

I sigh. "Not in the way you're implyin'."

"Don't make me sorry I'm doin' this, Miss."

"It's Missus. And the only reason you'd be sorry is if you wait too long to check on him."

Chapter 50

Dr. Gideon Box.

I CAN'T BELIEVE Renee's still awake. I stretched my dinner into an eighty-minute marathon, and kept her talking long enough that she's consumed an entire bottle of wine. With the cobbler finally gone, there's nothing left to do but paint her nails.

She positions herself on the bed, with four pillows propping her upper torso. She's still naked from the waist down. Her legs are spread apart to give me the full view of her orange, heart-shaped bush. But just above it, I've got another view. She's resting the butt of the gun on her stomach, aiming it point blank at my chest.

I open the nail polish, and paint her toe nails as slowly as humanly possible, hoping she'll fall asleep before I finish.

"You're being very meticulous," she says. "I like that."

"You know what else you might like?" I say.

"What's that, honey?"

"A foot massage."

That should put her to sleep and prevent me from having to receive detailed instructions in the art of giving oral to a crazy person.

"A foot massage," she says, dreamily. "How thoughtful. Yes, I'd like that, Darrell. Maybe we could do that after you kiss me. Down there."

Did she just call me Darrell?

She did.

And things start coming together for me.

I say, "It must have been quite a shock when Trudy and Darrell found out they were brother and sister."

She gives me a long look and says, "That sounds like a lot of information for a waitress to give during a dinner service. And since we're on the subject, I never believed for a minute my Daddy strung you up for pecking Trudy's cheek after bringing your meal."

"I have to admire your father. Scooter."

"Why?"

"If I found out my wife had a baby with another man, I'd probably resent her *and* the kid."

"That speaks to a character flaw in *you*, Gideon. A flaw you'll be able to correct, with my help."

"Scooter and Darrell have become very close, considering they're not related."

"My father's a loving, giving man."

"You know what I think?"

"What?"

"I think your father and Darrell helped you kill your husband and best friend. And then I think you returned the favor by killing Aunt Lori when she won the lottery."

"She died from cancer."

"From what I understand, Lori's cancer was in remission. I think you found a quicker way to get the money in Darrell's hands."

"Good luck proving that. Aunt Lori was cremated."

"You know what else I think?"

"What?"

"I think you hung Trudy's mother and made it look like an accident. And I don't think Scooter and Darrell know anything about that."

"Is that Trudy's theory?" she says.

I notice her eyelids are getting heavy. She's got to be drunk enough to pass out. If I can just keep her talking long enough, she'll drift off on her own, peacefully.

"Is that what Trudy thinks?" she says.

"No. It's what I think."

She closes her eyes for several seconds. Then opens them and says, "Anything else?"

"Yeah."

"Go ahead, then. Spill it all."

"I think somewhere along the line Darrell's done some toenail painting and bud blooming of his own."

She smiles. "I said it before. You've got a fine mind, Gideon. If true, there'd be no shame in it. Darrell and I aren't related."

"Except through marriage."

"You're quibbling."

"Am I right?" I say. "About everything I said?"

"If I did all those things, would it help you admire me?"

"Possibly."

"I wonder. Still, I doubt you'd admire someone foolish enough to admit to a crime."

"There are no police here. Just us."

"I think I'll let your theories about me remain unanswered. But I would like to know one thing."

"What's that?"

"How can you possibly believe I hung Lucy?"

"It's your father's execution method of choice."

"Maybe *he* hung her."

"I don't think so."

"You think I did it hoping to please him? If so, why wouldn't I tell him?"

"You couldn't. You had no way of knowing how he'd react to his daughter hanging his wife. I think you hung her for a different reason."

"I'd love to hear it."

"I think you grew up hating her, and blamed her for taking Scooter out of your life."

"I won't deny that. But why would I hang her?"

"To experience what your father feels when he hangs someone. You thought it would help you feel connected to him."

"I wonder if you'll try to run these theories past the police."

"You think I give a shit about any of those people? Your husband, your best friend, your Aunt Lori, your step-mother, Lucy?"

"I think you care about Trudy. And might want to share your feelings about how her mother died."

"I'll tell you the truth. I never had sex with Trudy. But we did kiss, and I felt her up over her clothes. That's it, and that's the truth. Yes, I was hoping for more. But Scooter came along and bashed me in the head, dragged me to a barn, and tried to hang me. The beam broke and brought half the roof down on top of us. I was uninjured, Scooter sustained a broken leg. End of story."

"My Daddy's leg is broken?"

"You didn't know?"

The look on her face says she didn't.

"I'm sorry," I say.

"For what?"

"He's in the hospital in Starbucks. And hasn't contacted you."

"He's probably still sedated."

"Renee, if there's one positive thing I can say for you, apart from your ability to kill, and your willingness to fuck total strangers, it's that you've got a wonderful, nurturing spirit."

"Thank you, Gideon."

"It must be hard on you to realize your father doesn't trust you to take care of him."

"He'll contact me when he gets out of the hospital," she says. "He always does, and always will."

"I hope you're right."

"We'll nurse him back to health in no time! You'll see."

"We?"

"You and me."

"The man tried to *hang* me. Why would I take care of him?"

"For one thing, you're a doctor. For another, you took an oath. For another, it would help you clear up this silly misunderstanding."

"What misunderstanding?"

"My father never tried to hang you."

"I've got a rope burn says you're wrong."

"What you've got is an active imagination. And imagination's a wonderful thing. It helps provide a context for our knowledge and experiences, and helps us make sense of the world around us."

"Do you ever get tired of hearing your voice?"

She sighs. "I've tried, Gideon. I really have. But while I've tried to bring you joy, you've treated me with contempt, and scorn."

"Does this mean you're ready to end our partnership?"

"I'm afraid so."

"Good. Because I'd rather bathe with pacus than be in a relationship with you."

"What are pacus?"

"Testicle-eating fish."

"You're just plain rude, aren't you?"

"I am for a fact. And you know why I'm comfortable saying all this?"

"No."

"Because you don't have the guts to shoot me."

"You honestly believe that?"

"Sort of," I say. "I mean, I know you're a cold-blooded murderer, and I'm certain you'd shoot me without batting an eye. But not here. Not now. There's no way you could explain it to the police. And it would open the door to closer scrutiny of your other crimes."

"So where does that put us?"

"I believe it allows me to walk out of here unscathed. Which is exactly what I plan to do."

I stand.

She raises the gun, aims it at my chest, and says, "Tell me again why I can't shoot you?"

"Because if you wound me, I'll give eye-witness testimony against you. And if you kill me, my corpse will put you away for the rest of your life. Face it, Renee, you're screwed."

She pulls the trigger.

Chapter 51

Trudy Lake.

AN HOUR PASSES before my cell phone rings. It's Detective Tan, from the Paducah police department.

"Is he all right?" I ask.

"Are you still in Starbucks? At the hospital?"

"Yes, sir."

"I need to talk with you, but I'd rather not do it on the phone."

"I'm still a patient, and I don't own a car."

"It's too late to do this now. Maybe I can come up there first thing in the morning."

"Sure, of course. Can you just tell me if Dr. Box is okay?"

"We're not sure."

"What's that mean?"

"He's missing. And so's his car."

"What about Renee?"

"I'm not at liberty to say. Not at this time."

"What about Dr. Box's cell phone?"

"That's a helluva good question, Miss. Hang on."

The line goes quiet for several minutes. Then he says, "That's missing too."

"Oh my God!" I shout. "Thank God!"

"Ma'am? Why is the missing cell phone such good news?"

"I'll see you tomorrow, Detective. And thanks for your help."

I terminate the call and answer the call that got me so excited.

"Gideon! Is that you?"

"It's me," he says.

"Are you okay?"

"Yes."

"Thank God."

"Trudy?"

"Yes?"

"Are you still open to the road trip?"

"If you would've asked me ninety minutes ago I'd have said yes in a heartbeat."

"But now?"

"Can I ask you four questions?"

"Yes. If I can ask you one."

"You'll have to answer honestly."

"You too."

"I'll start," I say. "First, did you fuck my sister today?"

"Yes."

I close my eyes, shake my head. "Why?"

"Is that your second question?"

"Yes. I had another one in case the answer was no."

"Okay. So the question is why did I have sex with your sister? The short answer is I didn't know Renee was your sister. The complete answer is she was one of three women I'd been writing to, on the internet for several weeks."

"Faith Hemphill, Renee Williams, and Zander Evans."

"How did you know?"

"Small towns, Gideon. People talk."

"Still."

"Question three. Where are you?"

"Less than a mile from you. In a motel."

"Why?"

"Is that question four?"

"No."

"I'll answer it anyway. I'm staying here tonight so I can see you tomorrow. And if you decide you want to come to New York with me, I'll keep staying here till you're ready to travel."

"Question four. What happened tonight? After you were cleared of the robbery."

"You know about the robbery?"

"Small towns, Gideon."

"Right. So anyway, I go back to my hotel room after being framed for robbing the bowling alley—"

"With Zander Evans—"

"Yes, and there's a knock at the door. I open it and—"

"It's my sister, Renee—"

"Right, and I can give you the long version tomorrow, but the short version is she wanted us to be a couple, and I found out she was your sister and I didn't want to see her anymore. She took it hard and pulled a gun on me. We got into an argument, and she tried to shoot me."

"Then what happened?"

"You've asked four questions."

"You never finished the fourth one."

"I told you she tried to shoot me."

"My question was 'what happened tonight?' You haven't told me the rest."

"She aimed the gun at me, pulled the trigger, nothing happened. She pulled the trigger again, and it clicked."

"Did she forget to load it?"

"No. It was a revolver. I could *see* the bullets. But they didn't fire."

"Renee knows how to shoot a gun."

"Believe me, she was more stunned than I was!"

"So what did you do?"

"I packed up my shit, grabbed my cell phone, and left her there."

"She didn't put up a fight to make you stay?"

"No."

"Weird."

"You think you can forgive me for having sex with your sister?"

"Is that your question?"

"No. Forget that one."

"Okay," I say, relieved. "What's your question?"

"Renee said you've got a history of handcuffing men to the fence behind the restaurant and blowing them. What I want to know is—"

"I'll have to call you back!" I say, and hang up.

That fucking Renee!

I take a deep breath, call him back and say, "Sorry about that. I can't really talk right now because Clem keeps poking his head in the door. I think we both have some explaining to do, and we can do it tomorrow, after the detective finishes talking to me."

"What detective?"

"The one from Paducah. He's driving here to meet me first thing in the morning."

"Why?"

"He wants to tell me something."

"About me?"

"I guess. Or Renee. Or both of you."

"Will you call me when he leaves?"

"Yes."

Chapter 52

Dr. Gideon Box.

THE DISPLAY ON my cell phone says Trudy's calling. I answer with, "Has the detective gone?"

"No. He wants to see you."

"Why?"

"He wants you to make a statement."

"With you there?"

"I don't know. Probably not. But I told him you were alive, and here in town."

"I can be there in five minutes," I say.

I get there, say hi to Trudy, and she introduces me to Detective Tan, who immediately takes me to the hospital chapel and records my statement. When that's done, he fills me in on what happened after I left the hotel.

Renee flew into a drunken rage and trashed the room. When the other hotel guests complained, the front desk called the room and got no answer. They sent a security guy to check things out. After knocking and getting no response, he opened the door with his pass key. Found Renee passed out on the bed with a gun beside her. Moments later a policeman showed up, thanks to Trudy's concern for my safety. When they try to rouse Renee, she babbles an amazing story about killing her husband and her best friend, strangling Aunt Lori, and lynching her step mother.

"I believe all those things are true," I say.

Detective Tan says, "So do I. But there's no proof, and drunk babbling does not a confession make."

"Why not?"

"The defense team will hire ten psychiatrists who'll swear that drunk people often confess to crimes they've never committed. And they're right. By way of example, my wife had too much to drink one night, and—I shit you not—confessed to killing Elvis."

"Maybe she did."

"She was eight months old when Elvis died."

"I'm assuming you didn't haul her ass to jail."

"No. And I won't be hauling Renee there, either."

"What about the gun?"

"She's got a permit. We're doing ballistics on it, but my guess is it'll come back clean."

"Why am I alive?"

"That I can't answer, assuming your story's true. If it is, you're one lucky son of a bitch."

I go back to Trudy's room and give her a kiss on the cheek.

"Is he bothering you, Trudy?" Clem says.

"Can you give us some privacy, Clem?" she says.

"No. My orders are to stay here the entire time he's in the room."

"That was when they were sortin' things out. They cleared Dr. Box of any wrong-doing. The only reason you're here is to protect me from Daddy and Darrell."

"Until the Sheriff himself changes my orders, I'll follow the ones I've been given."

She sighs.

I say, "Do we really care if he hears us talk?"

"Why wouldn't we?"

"It's a small town. Within an hour he'll know everything we said anyway."

"I don't care. I'm not answering any personal questions as long as he's in the room."

"I'll respect that. How much did the detective tell you?"

"A hell of a lot more than you did."

"Like what?"

"Like how you took a shower after letting Renee in the room because you wanted to get cleaned up for her after spending several hours in jail."

"*What?* How did he know that? I just told him five minutes ago! And anyway, there's a simple explanation for—"

"He also told me how you asked her to monitor the phone in case you received any important calls, and that's how she was able to call me, and of course there's the little part about how she ordered you a big room service dinner, and how you drank a bottle of wine together—"

"*She* drank the wine, I just—"

"And how you painted her toenails, and—"

"At *gunpoint!*"

"He said she was completely naked, and—"

"Just from the waist down!" I say, outraged.

"Can you hear how this might be taken the wrong way?"

"Yes, but—"

"He told me you got her drunk."

"Yes, but—"

"I'm so *proud* of you!"

"What? You are?"

"Oh, for the love of God!" Clem says, from his post, on the other side of the room.

"Shut up, Clem!" Trudy says. To me she says, "I've spent all night thinking about your offer, and I've decided if you're still interested, I'll go to New York City with you. On one condition."

"What's that?"

"We can't ask each other any questions about our past."

"That's nuts!"

"We start fresh. Beginning right now."

"I think I have a right to know what happened at the fence."

She sighs. "And I have a right to know what you were hoping to do with Zander at the riverbank, with your pants around your ankles. But you know what? I've got the good taste not to ask."

"That's a copout!" I say. "A one-time thing. From what I hear about the fence—"

"Gideon," she says. "Look at me."

I do as she says.

"Do you really care what happened at the fence?"

"Yes," I say. "Absolutely!"

"Is it more important than us? Think before answering."

I pause a moment.

And another.

Then say, "No."

She smiles. "Right answer. Now kiss me. Very gently."

I look for a place on her face that isn't swollen, bandaged, or bruised.

"Where?" I say.

"Surprise me."

Chapter 53

Trudy Lake.

BECAUSE OF DARRELL'S impendin' court date, and Daddy's hearin', and my continuin' divorce battle, I tell Gideon to go back to New York, and I'll meet him in two weeks. With Renee on the watch list of three county police departments, and Cletus and Renfro dead, and Darrell banged up to the point he can't blink his eyes without shittin' his pants, I reckon I'll be safe in Clayton till then.

Gideon wants to put me up in a hotel until my affairs are settled, but for the first time in my life I have an organized plan to move away, and I'm lookin' forward to packin' the items I'd like to take.

Gideon's worried about Daddy, but Daddy's not an issue. He's in Logan, bein' cared for by Renee. So it makes sense for me to stay in my own home for the next two weeks.

"I don't like it," he says, imitatin' Clem, to make me smile.

The hospital doctor works his way to my room around noon, and clears me to check out. An hour later, I'm sittin' in a wheel chair out front with an orderly at my side, squintin' against the harsh sunlight, waitin' for Gideon to drive up in his rental car and whisk me home.

When I'm settled in the car, he says, "Are you up for a short trip?"

"What do you have in mind?"

"I need to meet someone."

"Who?"

"Faith Hemphill."

"Are you *crazy?*"

"Yes. Absolutely. Why do you ask?"

I frown. "Is this gonna be a regular thing with you?"

"What?"

"The women, Gideon. Every time I turn around you're with one woman or another, and either her pants are off, or yours are around your ankles."

"This meeting's about you," he says.

"Me?"

"Yes."

"Well I've got no interest in meetin' her!"

"Why not?"

"Did you not drive two full hours a few days ago hopin' to bang her?"

"Yes. But I learned a valuable lesson that day, with her, Zander, and Renee."

"To keep your dick in your pants?"

"Yes."

"Promise it."

"As long as you're willing to stay with me, I promise to keep my dick in my pants."

I laugh.

"What?"

"You just basically promised we'll never have sex."

"I did?"

"Rewind it in your head."

He does. Then says, "That didn't come out right. I need a mulligan."

"Too late," I say. "You already made the promise."

Chapter 54

TURNS OUT WE'RE meeting Faith Hemphill at the half-way mark to her house because she has sea horses she can't leave for more than four hours at a time. When I see her I'm no longer jealous. She looks old enough to be Gideon's mom, and burly enough to play offensive tackle for the Tennessee Titans.

The reason we're meetin' Faith makes less sense than the idea of Gideon datin' her in the first place. She's here to sell him some sort of powder that can disable people, and make 'em crazy enough to shoot each other by mistake.

The three of us are standin' in a vacant lot where a gas station used to be. It's all hush-hush, like some sort of big-time drug deal.

Gideon says, "You brought the powder packets?"

Faith says, "You brought the cash?"

When they make the exchange I laugh out loud.

Faith raises her chin at me and says, "Is that her? The one you felt up?"

I say, "You told her that?"

"Renfro told me first," Faith says. She casts a careful eye on me and says, "You're puny." To Gideon, she says, "Couldn't a' taken you five seconds to feel whatever she's got in that little trainin' bra."

"At least I get measured for my bras," I say. "Instead of sur-veyed."

"Ladies, please!" Gideon says.

"Sorry," Faith says. "That was me bein' jealous."

"Me too," I say. "So, this powder really works?"

"Ask Cletus and Renfro," she says.

I walk over to her, and we shake hands.

"How does it work?" I say.

"You any good at chuckin' rocks?"

I smile. "What kind of country girl would I be if I couldn't chuck rocks?"

Faith says, "Gideon, walk away from us a minute."

When he gets about fifteen feet away, she calls him by name. He turns to look at us, and Faith hurls a dust bomb at him.

Gideon screams as it explodes on his chest.

Faith says, "Don't be such a pussy. That ain't nothin' but flour and bakin' soda."

"You could've warned me," Gideon says, slappin' the powder off his clothes.

She hands me a packet and says, "Now you try. Remember to fling it hard."

I hurl the packet at Gideon and he explodes into a cloud of flour for the second time.

"*Damn* it!" he shouts.

"Shouldn't I aim for the face?" I say.

"The chest is a bigger target. You hit a man's chest with the blindin' powder, it'll put him on the ground quick."

"What if he closes his eyes at the last second?"

"The glass and pepper dust hangs in the air. After a man's been hit, he'll open his eyes. It's a natural reaction. When he does, the glass and pepper gets in there and burns like hell. He'll rub his eyes to ease the pain, but what he's really doin' is rubbing ground glass into his eyeballs. It's brutal."

"I don't think I can do that to a person," I say.

"If your life's on the line you'll use it and wish you had more."

"On the bright side, everyone who wants to hurt me is either dead or hurt."

"I hope you're right. But I'm still keepin' the money Doc Box give me just now."

"You know what I think?"

"What?"

"I think Gideon was at your place when Cletus and Renfro broke in."

She gives Gideon a look and says, "Why would you think that?"

"My husband sent them to kill Gideon, not you. Dumb as they were, they would've known if his car was at your place. They wouldn't have broken into your house unless they knew he was in there."

"I expect you'll keep those thoughts to yourself," she says.

"What thoughts?" I say.

She smiles.

"I could learn to like you," she says.

"I already like you."

"Why's that?"

I point at Gideon.

We laugh.

"Kiss my ass!" he says.

"That's Trudy's job," Faith says, "though I don't know why she'd want it."

Chapter 55

"YOU BOUGHT TEN packets from her?" I say, after Faith leaves.

"I only wanted two, but she needs another tank."

"Is that supposed to make sense?" I say.

"Her seahorse tanks cost a thousand bucks each. She wouldn't sell me less than a thousand dollars' worth of powder."

"What'll you do with the other eight packets?"

"Keep them for our protection in the city. Can you imagine someone trying to mug us and getting a face full of blinding powder? It's a ridiculously effective weapon, with a shelf life of forever. And you don't need a permit to carry it."

"Sounds like you're in hog heaven."

"I feel like the caveman who discovered fire," he says.

"Powerful?"

"You know it."

"Maybe I'd respect that power more if you didn't look like the Pillsbury Dough Boy," I say.

"Right."

"Want some help gettin' that flour off your clothes?"

"All help would be greatly appreciated."

I start punchin' his back and sides.

"*Ow!*" he yells. "What the *hell?*"

"You seemed to take pleasure beatin' me up. I want to see if I get the same rush."

"Stop!"

"What's wrong?"

"I didn't enjoy hitting you. And I'll never do it again."

"I don't know. I haven't heard an apology yet."

"Apology? For what?"

"Uh...for *hittin'* me? Hello?"

"You *made* me do it."

"To save your ass from a felony assault charge."

He thinks about it a minute, then says, "You're right. You took all that pain for me, and

didn't have to. I think I've been looking at this from my own, selfish point of view. As usual."

"I'm listenin'," I say.

"I thought by running over Darrell I saved you from a much *worse* beating. But once Darrell was incapacitated, you could've let the police come to the barn and draw their own conclusions. And if that happened, they would've thrown in jail and Darrell would've had a legal case against me."

"You just *now* came to that conclusion?"

He says, "I'm sorry, Trudy."

"For?"

"For hitting you."

"You're forgiven. Now let's get you cleaned up."

"Okay, but slap, don't punch, okay?"

"Okay."

"Ouch! Shit! Slap my clothes, not my face!"

"Sorry."

When we get to my place, Gideon insists on checkin' each room. He makes sure all the doors and windows are locked. Peeks in the closets and under the beds. Here's a guy that came to town a few days ago thinkin' about no one but himself. Now he's practically dotin' on me.

I like it.

But he needs to get back to Nashville and catch a flight.

"I'll be fine," I say.

"Okay."

He reviews for the third time how he's booked a limo to drive here from Nashville to pick me up in two weeks. He gets on my computer and prints out the airline reservation and tells me how to check my bags.

"You've never flown before," he says. "I don't want you to be nervous."

"I'm not the least bit nervous. I'm excited!"

"The driver will take you to the airport. You're flying non-stop to LaGuardia Airport. When you get to the gate—"

"When I get to the gate, I'll go to baggage claim," I say. "You'll be standin' there with a limo driver. Got it. Now go on, before you miss your flight."

"I hate to leave you here without a car. How will you get to your attorney meetings and all the other places you'll need to be?"

"Kennon will drive me anywhere I need to go durin' the day. At night, while she's at work, I'll be right here, safe and sound."

"I wish you had neighbors."

"I've got neighbors on both sides."

"What, a mile away?"

"Quarter mile at most. I can run a sixty-second quarter, by the way."

He frowns, then hands me two packets of powder.

"Keep these in your back pocket at all times. If you have to use them outside, make sure the wind is at your back. Don't get within ten feet of the cloud it makes. Better yet, throw it and run the opposite way."

"Got it."

"I'm serious, Trudy. If the wind shifts, you're toast."

"Kiss me goodbye, Gideon. I'll see you in two weeks."

He kisses me, takes a long, last look, then leaves.

I stand at the door and watch him drive away.

When he's completely out of sight, I lock the door, turn on the livin' room fan to get the air circulatin', and start puttin' things in piles. These I'm throwin' away, these I'm givin' away, these I'm takin' with me to New York City. After a few hours of that, I go online, email some friends about my hospital adventure, tell 'em about Dr. Box, and how I'm goin' to New York City. Then I call Alice T's and tell Big Ed I'm quittin'.

"I could use you here these next two weeks," he says.

"With Scooter laid up and out of town, I'd be too skittish at closin' time," I say.

"Kennon could bring you like before, and I could drive you home."

"I couldn't let you do that. Plus, Dottie would skin us both."

He laughs. "She's right jealous, my wife. If you come in to say goodbye, I'll catch you up on your hours."

"Forget those few hours of pay, Ed. You've been more than fair with me. But I'll want a hug from you and the girls before runnin' off to New York."

"You're finally going to do it!" he says.

"I finally am."

"I know that's what you always wanted," he says, "and more power to you. But I'll miss you."

"I'll miss you, too, Ed."

I hang up, watch a little TV, make some dinner, eat, put the dishes up, walk back through the house to turn off the lights. When I get to the livin' room, I nearly jump out of my skin.

Sheriff Boyle's sittin' in Daddy's TV chair with his feet propped up like he owns the place, givin' me a look that says he ain't here on official police business. I start to reach into my back pocket, but stop when I realize the fan is runnin' full blast behind him. If I throw the powder at him it'll blow back on me.

"How'd you get in here?" I say.

"I've had a key to Scooter's place for years. And he's got a key to mine."

"Well, Scooter's not here."

"I wouldn't' be here if he was."

"What do you want?"

"*You.*"

Chapter 56

FOR A SPLIT second, I freeze. I think about askin' Sheriff Boyle what he means, but his meanin' couldn't possibly be more clear. He's starin' at me with dead eyes, like he's been drinkin' all afternoon and come to a snap decision.

"You need to go home, now, Sheriff. Luby's gonna be worried about you."

"Luby'll be just fine, Trudy."

"You've been drinkin'. You shouldn't be here."

"You have no idea what it's been like these two years. Seeing you sashay your sweet little ass all over town, hooking up with this loser or that one, always trying to get away, like our town isn't good enough for you. Then you hook up with a fuck up like Darrell, your own brother, and now you aim to run off with a guy old enough to be your father, who's my age, by the way."

"You need to head on home now, Sheriff, Luby'll have dinner waitin' on the table."

"What have you got for me, Trudy?"

"Excuse me?"

"You give it up for all these losers. I'm the law in this town. I'm the one who protects people. You let a total stranger feel you up at the fence? What about me?"

"You've already got a woman, Sheriff. And a fine one, at that."

He scrunches his face up and runs his fingers through his hair and says, "You send for me to come to the hospital last night like I'm some sort of errand boy, tell me how to run my business. Then you tell me to go fuck myself."

"Well, I'm sorry about that. I was frustrated. I definitely owe you an apology."

"You owe me a helluva lot more than that. I'm thinking of something pink."

"That's the drink talkin', Sheriff, not you. You need to think about Luby, and how this sort of talk would make her feel if she heard it."

"I was there that night you walked out on the football field to accept your award. Homecoming Queen." He sighs. "Most beautiful girl in five counties. Watching you grow up, seein' you make one bad decision after the other. I always showed you respect. But the way you treated me last night? I figured if half the town was getting in your pants, the Sheriff might as well get in there, too."

"First of all, you can count on one hand the men who've been in my pants, and when you do, you'll have four fingers left over. Whatever else you've heard is lies and speculation. I've done some things I'm not proud of, but Darrell's the only man I've been with in that way."

"Well, that's about to change," he says.

He pauses a few seconds, then bolts out of the chair and comes straight at me.

Chapter 57

I THINK ABOUT makin' a run for it, but there's no way I can get to the back door and unlock it before he can catch me. Instead, I grab a glass bookend from the book shelf.

"Good luck with that," he says.

He's quick and agile for bein' forty, but I've got plenty of experience dealin' with my own drunken addict, who enjoyed comin' at me when I denied him sex. I've got a clear shot, but that's the sucker move.

The one he's expectin'.

So I wind up, and fake a throw, knowin' he'll instinctively duck and cover up, just like Darrell.

He does.

When he looks back up, I hurl it into his forehead, and he goes down. I jump over his body, open the front door, and see somethin' that surprises me.

Cletus Renfro's car.

He must've taken it from the impoundment lot. Didn't want anyone to see his sheriff's car parked in my driveway.

I could easily outrun him, but not the car. I make the quick decision to get inside the car and hope the keys are in the ignition. I hear a noise behind me and turn to see Sheriff Boyle comin' out the door. He's hurt bad, and blood is literally squirtin' from the angry cut in his head. I run to the car, jump in the driver's seat, and lock the door. Unfortunately, all the windows are rolled down, and there's no time to roll them up. I look on the column to see if the keys are there, but they're not. I feel around on the floor board, but again, no keys.

I raise up, grab the packets from my back pocket, and wait for him to come into view on the driver's side. I can't throw both packets with accuracy, so I place one on the floorboard and scoot across the seat to give myself some room. When he stands at the driver's side he'll try to open the door, realize it's locked, and his focus will be on reachin' in and unlockin' the door. I'll hit him in the chest and scramble out the passenger door while shuttin' my eyes and holdin' my breath. Maybe I'll get lucky.

So that's the plan.

But it doesn't work.

When Sheriff Boyd gets to the door, he sees me windin' up, and when I hurl the packet, he somehow manages to duck out of the way.

It's dark, and I don't see the packet after it whizzes past him, but I know it's gonna land too far away to have any effect on him.

Now I'm tryin' to reach the packet I placed on the floor, but the Sheriff is all over me, grabbin' my legs, pullin' me toward him. He climbs half into the car to get to me, and lands a punch on my sore cheek that makes me so groggy and weak I can't do nothin' but be slid out the car.

I'm lyin' on the ground, and the only light I see is comin' from inside the car, where I see my second packet of powder has been crushed. Sheriff Boyd must have stepped on it while pullin' me out.

So I'm nine-tenths knocked out, I've got no weapons left, and I hear him openin' the trunk. I try to scream, but the sound that comes out of my throat is more like a scared, whimpering hiss.

Sheriff Boyd picks me up like a sack of flour, puts me over his shoulder, and dumps me into the trunk.

"Wh-what are you *doin'*?" I manage to say.

"I'm going to take you to my fishing camp," he says. "You've never been there, but it's real nice. You want the itinerary? I'm going to fuck you all night long. And when you're completely fucked out, I'm going to take you for a boat ride and sink you three hundred feet into the bottom of Kentucky Lake. By this time tomorrow, your pretty head will likely be in a catfish's belly, and your feminine parts will be working their way through the digestive tract of a giant paddlefish."

I get out a nice scream before he slams the trunk door shut, but I doubt it was loud enough for the neighbors to hear.

He starts the car and all I can think about is how lucky I am.

I take a minute to thank the good Lord for providin' such a hot night for my abduction, and for puttin' me in the trunk of a car with a broken air conditioner.

As he starts the car, I remove my blouse and tie it around my face.

Then brace myself for the comin' impact.

I feel the car backin' up, movin' slowly down the driveway. Feel it turn, stop, then lurch forward as Sheriff Boyd puts it in gear. Feel the right turn that leads to the open road. Feel the speed pick up. Hear the sheriff scream as the wind comin' through the open windows stirs up the blindin' powder on the floorboard. Feel the car losin' control. Feel it swerve off the road and pitch forward, as if we're goin' downhill. Feel it crash into somethin' sturdy.

Chapter 58

WHEN I OPEN my eyes I hear a lady's voice say, "Do you know where you are, sweetheart?"

I say, "If it ain't heaven, it's gotta be Starbucks."

"It's Starbucks County Hospital, dear," she says. "According to our records, this isn't your first time."

"I've never made it past Starbucks yet," I say, "though I've tried eight times."

"You were in a terrible automobile accident. It's a miracle you survived. You're a very fortunate young lady."

"What did we crash into?"

"I'm told you struck a tree."

"What about Sheriff Boyd?"

"He didn't make it." She pauses, then says, "I probably shouldn't have told you that. Were you close to the Sheriff?"

"Not really. But I think he was hopin' I'd open up to him more."

She nods. "He was a good man."

"He'll be missed," I say.

"Do you know your name, hon?"

"Trudy. Trudy Lake."

"Good. Now that you're awake, I'll go fetch the doctor."

"Wait. What about Sheriff Boyd?"

"He didn't make it."

"He's dead?"

"That's what I'm told."

She starts to leave.

"Wait," I say. "Am I okay?"

"You're fine dear."

"Did they take out my spleen?"

"Your spleen? No, hon. Why do you ask?"

"I dreamt they removed my spleen, and my husband, who's really my brother, mounted it above the bed, next to *his* spleen."

"Okay, hon, you're hallucinating. You won't even remember this conversation in a few minutes."

"The hell I won't!"

"I'll be right back."

"Wait!"

"Yes?"

"Has anyone contacted Dr. Box? From New York City?"

"Box? What sort of name is that? Just relax, Trudy. You're still groggy from the medication."

While waitin' for the doctor I try to remember what happened. It's just flashes right now, but I remember bein' real dizzy and scared. I was havin' trouble breathin'. Then I realized I still had my blouse tied around my head, and remembered the powder. I kept the shirt there in case the powder was still circulatin' after the wreck. I kept real still in case the sheriff was alive, and assumed someone would come along directly to offer help. But either time stood still, or everyone who passed by had somethin' else to do. After what seemed like a long time, I decided to try pushin' the trunk open. But when I reached up, all I felt was air.

The crash had popped the trunk open.

I staggered out, fell to the ground, and passed out for what might've been the second time. When I came to, I realized the car was on an embankment. That's why no one stopped to help. They couldn't see us. I made my way up the hill, then untied my blouse and put it on and tried to walk down the road. I don't remember anyone givin' me a ride to the hospital, but someone must have, 'cause here I am. I make a mental note to find the good person or people who helped me, so I can give them a proper thank you.

The doctor comes in and says, "I'm honored! You left at one o'clock this afternoon and missed us so much you went out and got a concussion less than twelve hours later. I believe that's a record. How do you feel, Trudy?"

"I can't feel my arms and legs. Is that the medication?"

"Excuse me? You've lost all sensation?"

"*I can't feel my arms and legs!*" I shout.

His face takes on a panicked look.

I wait a moment, then say, "I'm just havin' fun with you, doctor. I'm fine."

"Not funny, Miss Lake. Not funny at all."

The doctor's wrong. It *was* funny. I know because when I called Gideon and told him what I said, he laughed hysterically for a whole minute!

Then he said he'll be here in the mornin', and won't leave my side till we're safe in New York City. Then his voice takes on a smug tone as he says, "I was right about you being in danger, and I was right about the powder. Is there anything you'd like to say to me? Anything at all?"

"Yes."

"Go on."

I say, "I can't believe you fucked my sister!"

Then I hang up before he gets a chance to say anythin' else.

THE END

If you enjoyed "BOX," you'll love John Locke's Gideon Box novel titled, "Bad Doctor!"

***** WOW! *Bad Doctor* is a wild, jaw-dropping story that is so funny you'll laugh out loud. An amazing list of characters make every other book you read pale in comparison. I wanted it to go on for another 1,000 pages! A wonderful wild ride!

~ Ron Chicaferro (Scottsdale, AZ)

***** John Locke is a writing machine, cranking out multiple hit novels per year, and always entertaining me in the process. *Bad Doctor* introduces Dr. Gideon Box to the "Locke-verse," another colorful character with some amazing personality defects that make the reader love to hate him. I was able to breeze through this fast-paced novel in only a day, which is par for the course with Mr. Locke's novels.

~ Joe Barlow (Scranton, PA)

***** As of June 2012 I have read everything John Locke has published for Kindle. Every one of his novels is an easy read and will keep you entertained. "Bad Doctor" is a bit of a departure from Locke's series fiction, feature an antihero that you will either love or hate. I hope to read more books with this character.

~ James Bower (St. Louis, MO)

***** *Other 5 star reviews say it all. I'll just add: pure blast of entertainment, 10 on a scale of 1to 10, and I never pause even a moment of buying any new Locke book...*

~ David S. Drobner (Pembroke Pines, Florida)

***** *This is probably one of the most bizarre tales Mr. Locke has written, but then again maybe not. There are, as usual, some very colorful characters. And every time I think about the co-joined twin assassins, I just can't help but smile. It would just not be right if Rose didn't show up, and sure enough she does. Can't wait to read the good Doctor's next adventure.*

~ F. P. Right (NW PA)

***** *Just a great written story. I wish we could see more books on this main character.....*

~Thomas L. Wolford (Kent, WA)

***** *I have read everything of John Locke's that I can get my hands on and loved each one. I also have a great love for Donovan Creed, so much so, that I can definitely see the closeness of character between Dr. Gideon Box and Donovan. To me, it was a hilarious read. Most entertaining.*

~ Linda L. Roy (Louisiana)

***** *There is just nothing like a John Locke book! This is a brand new character, with a few old friends thrown in to thrill the faithful fans, but it has that Locke spin that no one else can give a book. As with everything John writes, it is a quick, fun, easy, entertaining read that makes you gasp one minute and laugh out loud the next. You start out hating this bad doctor but find out he has some redeeming qualities and really want him to come out on top in the* end. I read this book in one day, could not put it down and have now added Dr. Gideon Box to my list of favorite characters that I want more of.

~ Mary E (Minneapolis, MN)

***** WOW!!! Another great new character from John Locke. I read all of his books and loved them all and this book did not disappoint me.

~ K. Miles (Chandler, AZ)

***** A fun quick read, that will have you turning pages, as this evil doctor gets himself into all kinds of trouble. Completely twisted, humorous, campy fun! Can't wait for the next Dr. Gideon Box book. Thank you John Locke!

~ K. Parsley (Illinois, USA)

***** I have read every book that John Locke has written. Why? Because they are smart, creative and hilarious!

Bad Doctor is no exception. The only author I know to compare John Locke with is Nelson DeMille. The sarcastic humor and genius of John Carey is captured in each of Locke's novels. Gideon Box is no exception and you will embarrass yourself by laughing out loud, rolling on the floor in public.

Highly recommend and can't wait for John's next book!!!

~ Frank (Johns Creek, Georgia)

Preview . . .

BAD DOCTOR

John Locke

TELEMACHUS PRESS

Introduction

I

I'M DR. GIDEON Box.

If you're coming after me, don't do it in a hospital.

That's my domain.

And don't piss me off in the real world and expect a smooth hospital stay in the future, because I have a long memory, and no one is exempt. If you're not a patient but your loved ones are, I'll harass *them*.

Before you bully me in a bar, embarrass me on a date, or refuse to replace the shitty car you sold me, think about this: you'll never be more vulnerable in your life than when you're spending the night in a hospital. You're out of your element, drugged, and totally dependent on our schedules and personnel. When you're here, you're *not* family. You're prey!

Your wife just had a procedure and needs her sleep?

Good luck with that.

234

I'll swing by the nurse's station, make a notation on her chart. Every two hours someone will be in her room, waking her up, changing her IV, moving her around. If you're not guarding her closely I might slip in her room, flip her on her side, lift up her gown, check out her ass. Or maybe I'll feel her up while pretending to listen to her heart with my stethoscope.

Don't get me wrong. I have no interest in your wife's nude body. I'd only view or touch her because I can, and because it's another way to beat you.

You get what I'm saying?

Don't fuck with me.

II

I DIDN'T KILL Joe's mom last week.

I *could* have killed her, but one glance at her chart told me the hospital didn't need my help. Her catheter should have been removed a day earlier. Since it wasn't, I figured the nurses forgot it.

I was right.

Like ventilators, catheters are breeding grounds for infection. Sixty-five thousand patients a year die from infections caused by these two pieces of equipment.

I never knew Joe's mom, but thirty years ago Joe and I were on the sixth grade track team. A half-dozen of us were in the showers after practice the day Joe smacked my ass with a wet towel. I ignored it, but he kept smacking me. The others taunted me to do something about it. When I confronted Joe, he beat the shit out of me.

Picture me in a fetal position on the floor, clutching my stomach in agony. Now picture Joe and his friends pissing on me as a group, drenching me from head to toe.

Laughing.

Like I said, I didn't know Joe's mom, and didn't kill her.

But I let her die last week from an infection I could've prevented.

III

I'M NOT AN angel of mercy. I don't kill random patients.

I've got a list.

If you're on my list, it means you've done something I refuse to forgive. It's probably something minor to you, something you forgot long ago. But like the Stones said in the second best song they ever recorded, *time is on my side.*

Like everyone else in the world, you and your loved ones will eventually get sick or have an accident. And when you do, you better not come to *my* hospital, because I can kill you, maim you, infect you, humiliate you, frighten you, aggravate you, and generally fuck up your life in a thousand different ways.

Want an example?

I bet you didn't know that every year three hundred hospital patients burst into flames during routine operations.

Three hundred!

You think all those are *accidents?*

Thirty-six items in a standard operating room can explode under the right conditions. What I'm saying, I can turn your chest into a fireball using nothing more than an alcohol swab and a hot cautery device.

So don't piss me off.

And tread lightly, because I'm tightly wound. Every day it takes less and less to piss me off.

IV

I'M THE LAST guy you want to meet in the hospital—and *not* because I'm a vindictive son of a bitch.

I *am* a vindictive son of a bitch, but the reason you don't want to meet me is I'm your child's last hope for survival. When they wheel your kid into *my* operating room, it means his problems are so severe no one else can perform the surgery.

That's because I'm the most technically gifted congenital/cardiothoracic surgeon in the world.

That's right, in the *world*.

Think I'm bragging?

I'm not.

I take no pleasure in being the world's greatest surgeon.

Someone in the world makes the best flapjacks. Someone else is the best seamstress. And someone owns the world's biggest ranch, truck, or penis.

I'd rather be any of them.

Especially the guy with the biggest penis.

But it's my job to be the best surgeon.

My skill is my curse, and forces me to work in hell, under excruciating pressure. I say that and you think, yeah, there probably *is* a lot of stress in what I do, operating on infants and children.

No.

You think you know, but you don't.

You have no idea.

Want a glimpse into my world? That's me in the operating room, standing in the corner, crying silently so the others won't know. They think I'm psyching myself up for the six-hour procedure I'm about to perform.

See that tiny blue object on the table, surrounded by two highly-skilled nurses, a pediatric anesthesiologist, and assisting surgeon?

My patient, Lainey Sue Calfee.

Five pounds, less than a month old, structurally abnormal heart. It would take five minutes to tell you what's wrong with her, but she'll be dead by then. And anyway, those are only the problems I know about. You can bet I'll find more bad news when I open her chest in a few minutes.

I always do.

What you need to know about Lainey is she's not going to make it.

It's okay, I already told her parents.

V

THAT'S ME AN hour ago, approaching the conference room to meet Lainey's parents, Jordan and Will Calfee.

Of Calfee Coffee.

As I enter, Jordan and Will are on the sofa, grim-faced, holding hands. Nurse Sally's in the straight-back chair, giving me the evil eye. Security Joe's standing at the doorway.

As always, I nod at Security Joe and say, "Are you feeling okay? Because you don't look so good."

As always, he ignores me.

Jordan and Will jump to their feet, searching my eyes.

If my eyes could talk, they'd say I'm dying inside, thinking how the Calfee's lives will change forever when I kill their kid on my operating table.

Nurse Sally hates me. She's black, two hundred fifty pounds, her age a complete mystery. Could be forty, could be sixty. She's a wonderful, caring person, my polar opposite. She visits the parents before they meet me, warns them about my notoriously foul bedside manner, and attempts to calm them down after I leave.

Security Joe is mid-thirties, former Marine, big, tough, freaky quiet. The kind of guy you'd expect to see guarding the president.

Joe's chief of security, here to guard me from possible assault. He blends into the background, always ready to step between me and an angry parent. While Joe couldn't care less if I offend the parents, Sally constantly wants to slap me up the side of my head for doing so.

I'd love to have Nurse Sally's attitude, and probably would, if I had her job.

Or *any* other job.

I'm not asking for sympathy, but imagine if your job required you to do something that made you physically and mentally sick every time you did it. I know you can't relate, and there are no good examples, but you know that chalky stuff you have to drink the day before getting a colonoscopy? It tastes like hell and makes you shit for twelve hours straight?

Let's say your job was to drink that chalk every day of your life.

You'd like to quit, but you're the only one in the world who can do it, and every day you don't drink the chalk, a child you've met will die.

That's a lot of pressure.

After a few years, it gets to your head.

Makes you do crazy things in order to cope.

So that's what I do, perform one or two of these horrific, impossible operations, then go bat shit crazy and run out into the world and do stupid, dangerous things, like breaking into people's houses when they're on vacation, and assuming their lives.

VI

THE CALFEES ARE a young, pretty couple, with tons of money. This situation with Lainey Sue is probably the first bad thing that's ever happened to them that couldn't be solved with cash and a phone call.

After failing to find reassurance in my eyes, Jordan falls into her husband's arms and sobs.

I'd love to give this couple hope, but like I said, I don't get the easy cases. When I get the call it means a child's condition has passed critical. It means hope has left the building.

Like most dads before him, Will says, "We want Lainey Sue to have the finest treatment available. Spare no expense. Money's no object."

This probably impresses Jordan, but in my experience it's complete and utter bullshit.

After the fact, he'll complain about the bill, the access, the forms, rules and regulations, the nurses in the recovery unit, and everything else that inconveniences him in the slightest. He'll threaten to sue me and the hospital over our fees.

After all, I killed his kid. Why should he pay me two hundred grand?

Or I saved his kid, which means I did my job, like the world's greatest plumber does his job unclogging the family toilet.

So sure, the hospital and I deserve *something*, but two hundred grand?

How can we possibly charge two hundred grand for a days' work?

In most cases it's not even their money at stake, it's an insurance issue. But he'll threaten to sue over the deductible, or the overage, or the out-of-pocket, or the increased future premium assessment.

Before the operation we're all supposed to hold hands and be friends. Afterward, he won't give a rat's ass about me, or what I had to go through to save his child.

And neither will Jordan.

I don't say any of this to the Calfees, which proves I'm getting better at these parent conferences despite the stack of complaints in my personnel file.

"Everyone says you're the best," Jordan says. "I know it's bad, but you'll save Lainey, right? You will, won't you?"

When they beg, it's like I'm drinking the chalk. I'll need a toilet soon.

Jordan pulls away from her husband and gets right up in my face. Could there be any emotion on earth more raw and heartbreaking than a mother's love for her dying child? Jordan's red eyes and wet cheeks are love's battlefield. When she speaks, her hot, sweet breath fans my lips and fills my nostrils.

"Please, Dr. Box."

Despite the dire situation, despite Jordan's considerable beauty, wealth, and status, I see exactly what she wants me to see.

She's a good person.

By extension, her husband and daughter are good, worthy people.

Of course, I already know this.

She grips my wrist. "I need to know there's hope."

I glance at Nurse Sally's baleful look before responding. She's Mike Tyson in a dress, only angrier.

Sally's told me time and again the moms need something to cling to. Something to get them through the multi-hour ordeal that lies ahead. But I won't give any parent false hope. Sally knows this, but the look in her face says she's ready to leap across the room and royally fuck...me...up.

I ignore Sally's look as I always do, and tell Jordan what I tell all the moms.

"I'm sorry, Mrs. Calfee. There's no hope. You need to spend the next few hours adjusting to life without Lainey Sue."

Jordan backs away slowly, drops to the couch, stunned.

Nurse Sally shouts, "*Oh no, you didn't!*" And comes out of her chair like a rocket. She launches a meaty fist toward my throat. Joe steps between us, catches the blow on his forearm, and ushers me from the room.

VII

I DON'T HEAR what happens next, but the routine's always the same. The dads get angry. The moms cry. They demand to speak to the hospital administrator, Bruce Luce. They want a replacement surgeon, refusing to trust their child's operation to one who's already given up.

Bruce is on standby when I meet the parents, so he shows up quickly, finds Nurse Sally hugging Jordan to her ample bosom, Security Joe staring straight ahead with dead eyes while Will curses and threatens to physically assault me.

Bruce says, "We warned you in advance Dr. Box has a terrible bedside manner. He's a genius, not a communicator. But remember, he's never lost a patient at this hospital, or any other."

"Never?" they say.

"Around here he's called 'The Miracle,' and for good reason. Thirty-two hopeless cases. No fatalities."

"I don't like him!" Jordan says.

"I don't either," Bruce says. "In fact, I hate his guts. But he'll find a way to save Lainey."

"How could he stand there and say there's no hope?" Will asks.

"It takes the pressure off him to be perfect."

Nurse Sally pipes in, "The truth is Doc Box ain't fit to be in the company of man nor beast. The good Lord pulled every ounce of useful goodness outta that man at birth, and stuck a lump of coal where his heart should be."

"But?" Jordan says.

"But he's the one you want in that room with Lainey, because he never gives up. He'll fight the devil to save your child. And he *will* save her. But after he does, leave him be. Don't go looking for him. Don't try to thank him."

"Why?"

"This ain't a celebratin' sort of man. You've seen him at his best, not his worst. Trust me, you'll do well to leave him to his lonely miserableness."

Jordan and Will grudgingly sign off on the surgical procedure, and for the next six to eight hours, I reside in hell.

Of course, Lainey Sue died.

VIII

LAINEY SUE DIED several times on my table, but with her walnut-sized heart in my skilled hands, she came back to life again and again. You'd think this kid was Joan of Arc, the way she fought so valiantly! I got into it like I always do, hurling blood-curdling insults at my colleagues, my hospital, Lainey Sue, her innards, her parents, and even Calfee Coffee, which I actually like.

By the time it was over the nurses were sobbing with joy, and I'd gone through my entire repertoire of oaths and cuss words at least six times, having used them in every possible combination.

My hands were cramped beyond use, my nerves frayed, and the tendons in my back and neck were twisted and gnarled like Gordian Knots from the mental and physical exhaustion that comes from total concentration while standing in a precise position for hours at a time. Like always, the pain in my head felt life-threatening.

On the table, Lainey Sue was resting quietly, pink and fit.

Nurse Janet gushed, "What an amazing little girl! She absolutely refused to die!"

To me she said, "I'm filing a grievance against you for sexual harassment and verbal abuse."

"That's ridiculous," I said. "You've worked with me before. You know how I am."

"Never again. I'm done."

"We just saved a life here. Do you really care about a few cuss words?"

"You're getting worse."

"How?"

"You're a complete psychopath. You called me the C-word. You barked like a dog."

"Which C-word?"

"All of them. You called me things that didn't even make sense."

"I was in a zone!"

Nurse Margaret said, "She's right. I've never heard such vile language. You should be ashamed of yourself!"

She shook her head. "And the things you said to that poor child? And the *names* you called her?"

She crossed herself.

Then said, "You cursed like a drunken sailor, speaking in tongues."

IX

HOURS LATER, DESPITE the warnings, Jordan Calfee tracked me down in my office, threw her arms around me and said, "Omigod, you saved my daughter's life!"

Jordan had looked beautiful that morning. But now, standing in my office, she was positively radiant.

"Dr. Box! Gideon! You've given us a beautiful, healthy baby to raise!"

"Who let you in to see me?"

"Your secretary."

"Lola? Seriously?"

"Your fee, whatever it is, isn't enough. How can I possibly repay you?"

She seemed sincere.

I said, "Would you consider a blow job?"

Jordan paused a moment, as if her ears momentarily betrayed her. Then she slapped my face full-force, stormed out of my office, and reported me to Administrator Luce. She followed that up with a written statement to the hospital's board of directors, effectively earning me a four-day suspension and six months' probation.

We all would have preferred a harsher ruling, but there were two patients in the cue who would die if I'm not on duty when they're strong enough for surgery. One is Lilly Devereaux, whose parents, Austin and Dublin, offered to donate a wing to the hospital if I save their child's life.

Since Lilly's surgery will likely take place in five to seven days, the board voted to suspend me for four days, which would give them time to bribe our existing nurses to work with me, or hire new ones away from our competitors.

Secretary Lola said, "Now you'll have time to see Shelby Lynn."

"Who?"

She handed me a letter and said, "It's from the stack of fan mail I placed on your credenza last month."

"I've got fan mail?"

"You do."

I look at the letter. "You've read this?"

"I read them all. It'd do *you* good to read them, too."

"Why's that?"

"You're loved by many."

"Right."

Lola shrugged, left the room. I sat down, read the letter, then went home and booked the next flight to Cincinnati.

Chapter 1

Cincinnati, Ohio.
Thursday, 9:15 p.m.
Firefly Lounge.

"*DUDE!*" WILLOW SAYS, approaching. "Where've *you* been all my life?"

She stops two feet away, wearing a smile and very little else.

"Glenlivit 21, thirty bucks a shot, right?"

I glance at the dark amber liquid in my glass, then back at her.

She says, "We don't serve many of those. By the way, I'm Willow."

"Chris," I say. "Chris Fowler."

She laughs. "We don't use last names in here, Chris."

I nod.

"You're in the chair," she says. "Will I do?"

"Sure."

Of course she'll do. Willow's by far the class of the place. The problem is she knows it.

She flashes me the smile that earns more in tips than hookers get for a toss. It's a spectacular smile, well worth the fortune her parents must've spent on braces a few years back.

I wonder how proud they'd be to see Willow giving lap dances.

She hikes a leg over mine, taking care not to injure me with her five-inch stiletto. Her panties, blood-spatter red to match the shoes, hug her crotch so tightly they could pass for spray-on. Her cropped tee is bright white.

She's on my lap now, facing me, our eyes two feet apart. Mine black, hers, goldenrod.

I sip my drink. "Want one?"

"What, a Scotch?"

She laughs. "I wouldn't know it from lighter fluid."

I place the drink on the table beside us.

Willow says, "You want me facing, or turned away?"

"Facing. I like your smile."

"Then we're good."

She closes her eyes half-mast, pouts her lips, shows me her sultry look.

"You ready?" she purrs.

"What, no music?"

"DJ's cuing it. I could've waited another thirty seconds, but you're too cute. One of the other girls might've stolen you."

Right, stolen me.

Because I'm so cute.

To keep the conversation going I ask, "What do *you* drink?"

"Vodka cranberry."

"Can I buy you one of those?"

"Not here. You know, it's—"

"Against the rules?"

She laughs. "Against the law, actually."

"Why's that?"

"I'm underage. For liquor, anyway."

"Seriously?"

"I know," she says. "Weird, right?"

The music starts. Willow arches her back, lifts her chin, lowers it, raises it again, licks her lips seductively, then removes her top.

"Show time," she says.

She puts her hands high over her head and gives her tits a shake. Then leans into me, brushes her nipples across my lips and says, "You like that, sugar?"

"I do. Thanks."

She gives me an odd look and does that boobs-across-my-lips thing again, expecting me to kiss them, but I don't.

I picture her ten minutes from now, telling her friend, Cameron about it. She'll say, "See the older guy in the corner? Black jeans, t-shirt? I was grinding him just now, really working it. I rubbed my tits in his face and asked if he liked it, and guess what he said?"

Cameron will shrug.

"He said, 'Thanks.'"

They'll laugh, probably snort a line.

Cameron will ask how much I tipped.

"Two hundred."

"No shit?" Cameron will say.

Next time they come out, I'll completely ignore Willow and signal Cameron to come over. They'll exchange a glance, but really, what can Willow do? She can't claim I'm her customer if I ask for someone else.

It's just that no one, especially Willow, expects me to ditch her for Cameron.

If Willow's a solid eight, Cameron's a barely-five. But she'll do her best, and hope to earn a Franklin, or at least a Jackson. I'll compliment the hell out of her, act like I'm really into it, then I'll pretend to have an accident. They love it when that happens. Builds their confidence, makes them feel sexier than the others.

I'll tip Cameron four hundred for a twenty dollar lap dance.

All part of the plan.

Cameron will tell Willow I came in my pants and gave her four hundred bucks.

Willow won't understand. She'll flirt, try to get my attention. But I'll ignore her, break her confidence.

Women want what they can't have. Even dancers like Willow, who think they're hot shit.

The music ends, and I hand Willow the two hundred.

She smiles and says, "Thanks, Jimmy."

"Chris," I say.

Willow smiles and tosses her head the way pretty women do when they know you want them. She walks away, confident my eyes are on her ass.

Thanks Jimmy, she'd said, all matter-of-fact.

Like it's every day she gets two hundred bucks for a lap dance.

In her mind she's got me right where she wants me.

I can't wait to see her face when she hears about Cameron's tip.

Chapter 2

"OH MY GOD, you were incredible!" Willow gushes, three hours later. "Best sex I ever had!"

I'm lying.

I mean, yeah, we had sex, and I did my part, but Willow was barely involved.

She's lying on the bed, on her side, her back toward me. When she's sure I'm done, she moves forward till I slide out of her. She sits up, wipes herself with the bed sheet, and turns to watch me remove the condom and set it on the nightstand.

She regards it with disgust. Then gives me the same look.

Makes sense.

She's eighteen, I'm forty-two. It *is* disgusting.

From her perspective.

I prop a pillow beneath my neck and settle in to relax, but catch her looking away, and take the opportunity to suddenly lift my head and kiss her boob.

She recoils when she realizes my lips touched her skin. Now she's glaring at me to show how she feels about the unwelcome assault.

I lean back onto the pillow and stare at her in the lamplight. This is where I'd tell her she's beautiful, if I thought she gave a shit what I thought.

She *is* beautiful, though.

"Mind if I light one?" she says.

"I'd rather you didn't."

Willow frowns. She's not happy, but she'll get over it. She's two grand richer than she was ten minutes ago.

"Is this what you do?" she says.

"What?"

"Go from club to club, trolling for sex?"

"I would if I could. But my wife rarely leaves town."

"She's not coming home tonight, is she?"

"No. She won't be home till noon tomorrow."

"You don't act like a first-timer," she says.

"I've been to clubs before, but never asked anyone to follow me home."

"I'm honored," she says, sounding anything but.

Willow's making small talk, waiting it out. She's been paid a huge sum for ten minutes of talk, five minutes of sex. She figures I expect an hour for my cash, and she'll mentally calculate it before attempting her escape.

"You got a boyfriend?" I ask.

"Yes."

She's telling the truth. She and Bobby Mitchell live together in an apartment on Dillingham. She doesn't know I know this.

Mitchell is a local tough guy. Hangs out at Shady's Bar & Grill, a block from their apartment.

"You love him?" I ask.

She frowns. "Can we talk about something else?"

She regrets fucking me. Wishes she could just leave and put this behind her. But two grand's a lot of money for her to ditch me less than twenty minutes into the date. And even though she hated every minute of the sex, it's crossing her mind this could be an easy way to make some serious coin whenever my wife's out of town.

"I've never done this before," she says.

"I believe you."

I *do* believe her. Willow doesn't fuck well enough to be a hooker. As a lap dancer she earns enough to put gas in her car, food and drugs on the table, keep Bobby happily unemployed, the bills paid, and the landlord at bay.

Which puts her head and shoulders above the women I've dated.

She may be a lap dancer, but she's classy. She only wound up in bed with me because I manipulated her. I kept flashing money and pressing her buttons and managed to turn the entire evening into a competition between her and Cameron, one that Willow's ego refused to let her lose.

"I shouldn't have done this," she says, gathering her clothes.

"You needed the cash."

She steps into her panties, pulls on her jeans, dons her sweat-shirt.

"Bad decision," she says.

"Don't beat yourself up about it," I say. "It was only a few minutes out of your life."

"I could get fired," she says, trying to make me feel guilty. Like she's the first lap dancer who ever fucked a client.

She's dressed now, sitting on the bed, staring into space.

I know what she's doing, reliving the events of the evening, trying to figure out how it got to this point.

She turns to look me in the eyes. It's starting to hit her, the way I played her tonight.

"Nice job," she says. "Asshole."

"You're taking this awfully hard," I say.

"I feel like a fool."

"Willow. You're adorable. Sweet. Beautiful."

She says nothing.

I add, "This has been an honor for me."

"I hate myself," she says. "I want to vomit."

I sit up and say, "This is too much. I was hoping for an encore, but it's clear you've had a change of heart. How about you and Cameron switch places?"

Cameron jumps up from the over-stuffed chair where I'd paid her five hundred to sit and wait.

Willow says, "Are you *serious*? You want to fuck my *friend*?"

"I do."

"Then fuck you *both*! I'm *leaving*!"

To Cameron I say, "If you can talk your friend into waiting another fifteen minutes, I'll give you three thousand dollars. I would've given Willow the extra money, but she's had second thoughts."

"*Fuck you!*" Willow shouts. She grabs her purse, starts stomping off.

"Willow?" Cameron says, her voice pleading.

Willow stops, sighs, and turns around.

"What?"

"Please?" Cameron says.

Three grand's enough to change Cameron's life. For a woman with her looks, it's three months of lap dances. Willow knows this, and they're friends. But for Willow, it's just one more humiliation. Her cheeks are in flames. She's angry as hell. Had no idea I was good for another three grand tonight, and realizes she just pouted it away.

When Willow speaks, it's to me. "You expect me to sit here and watch you fuck my *friend*? For more money than you paid *me*?"

"You don't have to watch," I say. "But you have to stay in the room."

Her withering look incorporates the full monty of teenage attitude. "You don't *trust* me?"

"It's not personal. I don't know you well enough yet."

"You just *fucked* me!" she says.

"Yes. But we agreed you only did it for the money. I'm not calling you a thief, but wouldn't you agree more women would steal a man's money than fuck him for cash?"

Willow's look says I'm a cockroach to her. She's furious. So pissed, her body's shaking.

Realizing how close her friend is to leaving, Cameron's in full panic mode. She crosses the floor and whispers in Willow's ear.

I know what she's doing, offering to split the money. Fifteen hundred for *not* having sex is a pretty good deal. Willow agrees, and reluctantly crosses the floor to the comfy chair. She curls up in it and flips me the finger, then leans her head on one of the massive arms and closes her eyes.

Cameron waits for all this to transpire, then turns toward me and approaches the bed. When she's three feet away she plants her feet and starts swaying slowly, from side to side, shows me a goofy grin, and starts to strip.

They all do that.

I don't care how old they are, first time a woman strips in front of you, she'll get a goofy grin on her face and sway her hips like she's moving to music.

Usually the routine works for me, but Cameron's all arms and legs, tall, and skinny as hell. Except for her hair, she could be Popeye's girlfriend, Olive Oyl. And though it's an odd comment to make about a lap dancer, movement doesn't become her.

So I focus on her hair.

Thick, shoulder-length, brown, with auburn highlights.

Cameron takes her sweet time letting me see what's under her clothes. That's fine, I need time to reload. When she's naked she motions me to lie on my back. When I do, she climbs on the bed, straddles me, and works me inside her. My first thrust forces a sound from her throat that's meant to be sexy, but puts me in mind of a cow caught up in a breached birth.

Willow laughs in the background, despite her anger.

I bite my lip to keep from sharing the laugh.

Cameron's short on experience, and her porn star imitation grates on me like Porky Pig reciting Shakespeare. But for no other reason than to piss Willow off further, I pretend I love it. I moan and groan, and thrash about under Cameron and carry on like she's the lay of my life. Of course, this encourages Cameron, who, bless her heart, starts getting into it. She makes a sudden awkward move and we disengage. Undaunted, she pretends she meant for that to happen, and throws herself on her back, spreads her legs wide and yells, "*Do me*, Chris! *Do* me!"

I scramble to my knees and notice her legs are so long they actually span the king-size bed! I focus on the triangle in the middle, and try to climb aboard, but she bucks her hips repeatedly. After thirty seconds of this bullshit, I press my hand against her lower abdomen and pin her to the bed long enough to get inside her. This time she emits a high-pitched wail and starts chuffing while flailing her long, skinny arms and legs in all directions.

Can you picture this?

It's like trying to fuck an octopus in a windstorm.

Personal Message from John Locke:

I love writing books! But what I love even more is hearing from readers. If you enjoyed this or any of my other books, it would mean the world to me if you'd send a short email to introduce yourself and say hi. I always personally respond to my readers.

I would also love to put you on my mailing list to receive notifications about future books, updates, and contests.

Please visit my website http://www.donovancreed.com and contact me so I can personally thank you for trying my books.

John Locke

New York Times Best Selling Author
#1 Best Selling Author on Amazon Kindle

Donovan Creed Series:
Lethal People
Lethal Experiment
Saving Rachel
Now & Then
Wish List
A Girl Like You
Vegas Moon
The Love You Crave
Maybe
Callie's Last Dance

Emmett Love Series:
Follow the Stone
Don't Poke the Bear
Emmett & Gentry

Dani Ripper Series:
Call Me

Dr. Gideon Box Series:
Bad Doctor
BOX

Non-Fiction:
How I Sold 1 Million eBooks in 5 Months!